"I want to ask if you will deliver a package for me in Majorca, it's imperative that it be there before the fifteenth.

"There may be people after this. People who will try to take it from you if they put two and two together, if they learn for instance that you also go to Majorca, and that we sat at the same table."

"People?" she asked with a frown. "What kind of people?"

"I am forced to tell you. They will be enemy agents."

She stared at him incredulously. "Are you serious?" she demanded. When he nodded she said, "But how impossibly melodramatic. Who are you? And why me?"

He said simply, "It doesn't matter who I am, except that I'm beginning to suspect that I'll not get through to Majorca. . . ."

By Dorothy Gilman
*Published by Fawcett Books:*

UNCERTAIN VOYAGE
A NUN IN THE CLOSET
THE CLAIRVOYANT COUNTESS
THE TIGHTROPE WALKER
INCIDENT AT BADAMYÂ
CARAVAN
THE BELLS OF FREEDOM
THE MAZE IN THE HEART OF THE CASTLE
GIRL IN BUCKSKIN

*The Mrs. Pollifax series*
THE UNEXPECTED MRS. POLLIFAX
THE AMAZING MRS. POLLIFAX
THE ELUSIVE MRS. POLLIFAX
A PALM FOR MRS. POLLIFAX
MRS. POLLIFAX ON SAFARI
MRS. POLLIFAX ON THE CHINA STATION
MRS. POLLIFAX AND THE HONG KONG BUDDHA
MRS. POLLIFAX AND THE GOLDEN TRIANGLE
MRS. POLLIFAX AND THE WHIRLING DERVISH
MRS. POLLIFAX AND THE SECOND THIEF
MRS. POLLIFAX PURSUED
MRS. POLLIFAX AND THE LION KILLER

*Nonfiction*
A NEW KIND OF COUNTRY

# UNCERTAIN VOYAGE

# Dorothy Gilman

FAWCETT CREST • NEW YORK

A Fawcett Crest Book
Published by Ballantine Books
Copyright © 1967 by Dorothy Gilman Butters

http://www.randomhouse.com

Library of Congress Catalog Card Number: 67-20921

ISBN 0-449-21628-4

Printed in Canada

First Ballantine Books Edition: December 1988

20   19   18   17   16   15   14

To Patricia Schartle,
Agent Extraordinaire

1

THE SHIP HAD BEEN FIVE DAYS AT SEA, AND NOW MELISSA could feel tension rising in her at thought of their arrival the next morning in Cherbourg and a few hours later at Southampton; for on the following day, Sunday, they would reach Bremerhaven, Germany, and there she would be abandoned, rendered up to a huge and totally new continent—a crocodile with open jaws—where not a friend or acquaintance, not even a name scrawled on a slip of paper, would be available to her for the next fourteen days. It felt to her like a great void into which she must disappear, and even if she emerged from it unscathed a century later her intelligence grasped the fact that she could never emerge unchanged. All that she carried with her was herself—whoever and whatever that might be—and the two sheets of white paper upon which her travel agent had typed a complicated list of dates, names of hotels, and plane and train departures. It was not enough; she was terrified, and at times the terror rose in her like vomit.

"Yes, hello, how are you?" she called out, smiling, as

she passed the Fergusons who occupied deck chairs next to
hers on sunny days. Self-consciously she quickened her
stride, walking more purposefully so that no one would
guess her growing subterranean panic.

She had been nearly as frightened when she boarded the
ship in New York, but with the difference that at any moment before the ship sailed she could change her mind,
turn and leave, run home to safety and to Dr. Szym. Now
there was no turning back, for an ocean lay between her
and home, and while it crossed her mind that she could
disembark in Bremerhaven and ask for an immediate flight
back to New York, she knew that she had neither the courage nor the experience even to grapple with a change of
those authoritative black words in her itinerary. She felt
powerless to change anything, and least of all the brief
flare of braveness that had brought her here despite her
terror. Surely, she thought, Dr. Szym would not have allowed her to come if there was danger of her cracking?

She reached A deck and pushed open the door against
the wind. The sun was shining but there were no bikinis
today; people huddled under blankets in chairs, their heads
wrapped in bizarre, makeshift coverings—newspapers,
shawls, scarfs—so that they had the look of convalescents
placed under the sun by attendants. Melissa reached the
railing and clung to it, bracing her body against the wind.
Below, the sea boiled gray and white against the prow of
the ship. To the left and to the right stretched the limitless
space of the ocean, constantly, eternally streaming past in
its steady course toward infinity. It was the first time that
she had crossed an ocean, and its unbounded space continued to grip her with a strange excitement, the ship feeling a
small, man-made intrusion upon its surface, a microcosm
daring to cross the unsteady floor of the world.

She turned to look at the people around her and instinc-
tively her glance sought out the couples, the higgledy-
piggledy mismatched people whom she had watched in
wonder since the ship left New York. There was this constant procession of life aboard ship that she could not quite
capture for herself because she was alone; because almost

everyone else had someone—they had each other—and there had been no one with whom she could become a pair. She had hoped there might be. She could not mourn her marriage, which had ended irrevocably a month ago, but what she longed for, she knew wistfully, was the appearance of that man she ought to have married, the man who would have been waiting for her if she had not eloped at sixteen out of a desperate need to attach herself to life.

Across the deck, leaning against the side rail, she saw the man called Stearns puffing on his pipe and staring out to sea. Of the six people assigned to table 43 in the dining room he was the only one who did not enter into conversation or mingle with the others and she wondered about him because he also traveled alone. He gave no evidence of need. He appeared utterly self-sustaining, calm and deliberate, yet Melissa had begun to picture everyone whom she met as joined to others by invisible strings of dependency that kept them upright, smiling, and stable. Her own cords had been severed, leaving her no one, and out of this had come this vision of threads running from each person to unseen mothers, fathers, lovers, sisters, brothers, and friends, giving them nourishment and security like secret umbilical cords. Surely even this man Stearns depended upon someone, she reflected; in everyone's life there had to be someone, didn't there?

She glanced at her watch and noted with a sense of deep relief that it was nearing half-past seven, the dinner hour. There was just time to shower and change into her most attractive new dress, and she turned and fought her way back to the door, her melancholy lifting at the thought of something concrete to do.

But it was different tonight, already change was invading the long dining table, which until now had been a mainstay for Melissa and the high point of each day. The college students, whose wit enlivened each meal, were to disembark in the morning and they had brought centimes and francs to the table to discuss and memorize. Melissa realized with a pang that tomorrow night they would be

spending these same coins in Paris. Already they were
looking forward, they were no longer immersed in the
present to which Melissa had to cling for the sake of sanity.
It was true that twenty-four hours from now she would still
be seated at this same table but she would be entirely
alone, the sole survivor of two ports of call. And beyond
that—to the possibility of leaving this ship—she dared not
think; it was like trying to envision a landing on the moon,
too remote, too unreal even to consider.

Four of them arose from their dessert and with gay remarks went off to their evening, leaving only the man
Stearns seated at the opposite end of the table. Melissa lit a
cigarette, determined to linger over coffee no matter what
inconvenience to the waiters or to Stearns. It looked a long
evening ahead and she could sense the imminence of a
left-out-of-life feeling.

Stearns suddenly turned his head and looked at her. He
said, "I heard you say that you are going to visit Majorca."

She nodded. "Yes. I go first to Copenhagen for a few
days, and then Paris and then to Majorca."

"To Palma?" When she nodded again he said, "When?"
He seemed very serious.

"About the eleventh, I think; the eleventh of July. It's
the last stop before I fly home on the fifteenth. Are you
going there, too?" she asked curiously.

He crushed his cigarette into the ashtray. "I wonder if
you would meet me on A deck later, say at ten o'clock.
There is something I should like to ask of you. It's rather
important. Would you mind?"

She looked at him in astonishment. He had scarcely
spoken to her before, and perhaps because of this she had
labeled him dull. Now he wanted her to meet him on A
deck. She blushed. She had not been aware of any overt
admiration on his part except—now that she thought of
it—she had noticed him once or twice studying her ap-
praisingly. He had said very little at meals, in fact he had
seemed to her a complete cipher as a personality; but his
invitation made him at once mysterious and possible.

"Why not?" she said charmingly, with an expressive little shrug of her shoulders.

"Good—thank you," he said, and with a nod excused himself and left the table.

"Well! I have an assignation," she thought brightly, and she felt intrigued, happy, lighter. When she thought about the man she remembered that his eyes were a very pleasing shade of blue although it was a pity his cheeks were pitted with the scars of acne or smallpox. He could not be more than forty. "Oh damn," she thought suddenly, "I'm making images again, he'll be Prince Charming himself before ten o'clock arrives." It was what she had done with Charles, she knew now; she had needed him, and so deeply that she had ruthlessly fitted him into a pre-conceived image and then spent the years of their marriage burying Truth to preserve Illusion.

"But—well, really, anything can happen!" she thought delightedly, and enlarging on this, she imagined Stearns telling her that he had fallen madly in love with her: *There is a quality about you*, he would say in a bemused voice. *I have met other women more beautiful, but there is something so real, so genuine about you.* That would be nice, she thought, she would like to be real. Then he would of course apologize for being so impulsive but he would point out that if he did not speak now he would never see her again—he too was to disembark at Cherbourg, she remembered. It was her address that he wanted ("there is something I should like to ask of you") so that he could find her again when they both returned to America. She thought solemnly, "Doctor Szym was quite right, it can be a wonderful world if one is open to new experiences and not afraid!"

She finished her coffee—it was nearly nine—and withdrew to the writing room to address a few cards. Then she returned to her cabin to powder her nose and put on her trench coat. Very dimly from this distance she could hear the sounds of the orchestra in the ball room and she thought, drawing a new mouth with lipstick, "Perhaps he will ask me to dance. He may even kiss me." A feeling of deep excitement filled her. It was possible that now, at last, her life might begin, and snatching up her cigarettes and purse she hurried out and up the stairs.

There had been a withdrawal of light from A deck but the wind was still blowing hard, the seas running high and fast past the ship. The sky was gray—it was only twilight on the ocean—with clouds of leaden charcoal skidding across the sky, leaving wisps like smoke behind them. Yet perversely there was one star twinkling among the clouds, one bright solitary little star that looked so friendly it caught at Melissa's heart, for she longed quite desperately to shine with just such brightness in her loneliness. It was what she must—had to—achieve, it was the whole purpose of her trip. Leaning against the rail she closed her eyes and like a child whispered, "Star light star bright first star I've seen tonight, wish I may, wish I might . . ."

She felt the man come and stand beside her. Opening her eyes she turned and said lightly, "Good evening!"

He said quickly, almost breathlessly, "I won't take but a moment of your time—"

"But I have lots of time," she told him with a little laugh.

"I haven't," he said, and so bruskly that she stiffened. "I want to ask if you will deliver a package for me in Majorca, it's imperative that it be there before the fifteenth."

Deliver a package for him . . . There was dancing downstairs and he wanted her to deliver a package . . . She felt a wave of disillusionment overwhelm and defeat her so that for a moment she and the depressed sky became one. "You want what?" she asked incredulously.

"It's an imposition, I know, but it's terribly important. Can you do it?"

She shivered. He would never know how chilled, how rejected and rebuffed she felt. It was really vicious of him to make a useful object of her when she had anticipated so much from him. She wondered bitterly when she would stop believing in Santa Claus. "I suppose I could," she told him coldly.

"It's an extremely valuable package," he said, and turned to look into her face as if to impress this fact upon her.

"Very large?" she asked, to preserve the amenities and to prove both her civility and her practical sense. Nevertheless she did not like him; she could not *forgive* him.

"Quite small. It's a book." Glancing first behind him, he brought from his trench coat a thin flat package wrapped in plain white paper and tied with string.

"A book," she repeated dully, and then, suspiciously, "How do I know it's not heroin or something illegal?"

"You may open it if you like," he said. "The place to which you deliver it—do you mind memorizing it?—is a small shop in downtown Palma. Its name is the Anglo-Majorcan Export Company."

"Anglo-Majorcan Export Company," she echoed indifferently, and thrust the package into her pocket.

"The address is more difficult. Number 11, Plaza Veri Rosario."

"Number 11, Plaza Veri Rosario."

"You must tell them the key to what they want is on page 191. There is a message, too: tell them George is very sick. Look here," he added suddenly, "there may be people after this. People who will try to take it from you if they put two and two together, if they learn for instance that you also go to Majorca, and that we sat at the same table."

"People?" she asked with a frown. "What kind of people?"

"I am forced to tell you. They will be enemy agents."

She stared at him incredulously, her attention diverted at last. "Are you serious?" she demanded. When he nodded she said, "But how impossibly melodramatic. Who are you? And why me?"

He said simply, "It doesn't matter who I am, except that I'm beginning to suspect that I'll not get through to Majorca."

The bleakness of his statement impinged upon her fantasies. Something almost like compassion touched her and she gasped. "But you mustn't think that."

He gave a short laugh. "I'm a realist."

The word chilled her. "I'm not a realist," she said suddenly and impulsively. "I thought—I hoped—you wanted to see me, and all you wanted was to give me a book." As soon as she said this she knew it was the height of gaucherie; he looked at her as if she was quite mad—as indeed she was, struggling to find and grasp reality after so many years of unreality. But she should not have let the words slip; they betrayed her.

He said urgently, placing a hand on her arm, "I may not see you at breakfast, and I mustn't be seen talking to you here. You understand this is of enormous value? You'll deliver it?"

She nodded, caught and touched by his urgency which at the same time struck her as ludicrous. "Don't worry," she told him reassuringly, for wasn't reassurance what everyone wanted?

He left as suddenly as he had come, and again she was alone under that arc of boundless sky, alone in the universe, in this whole bloody universe of which she was only one small and struggling atom filled with energy and problems. "How many different cognitive worlds there are," she thought, staring somberly at the moving clouds. "I'm not really heartless, that poor man may actually be running for his life—why didn't it seem real to me? All I know is that I hoped he would ask me to dance, and he wants me to deliver a book." She shook her head at the absurdity of this world she had newly entered and then, perversely, felt laughter stir inside of her. These damnable needs of hers! Actually, and upon second thought—if everything was a matter of attitude, as Dr. Szym suggested—it should be a lark to meet a secret agent, and under different circumstances she might even find it so, but not now, not when she felt so alone and defenseless. If only she'd not said what she said to him! Her face burned at the words that had leaped involuntarily from her lips, and at what he must think of her for having misunderstood his invitation!

She decided to go to bed—it was lonely here now—and she walked down to her cabin and locked the door behind her. The music was a mockery to her now. She glanced only once at the package as she shoved it into the bottom of her suitcase but already it bore no interest for her because the encounter had not been—well, reassuring. It had taken something from her, diminished her confidence, her sense of value. She'd made a fool of herself—she knew it even if he didn't—and it was better to put it out of her thoughts lest she conclude again that reality was a world she dared not inhabit.

# 2

THEY REACHED BREMERHAVEN AN HOUR LATE, AND SUD-
denly Melissa found it difficult to endure the suspense and
wanted an end to it. The ship was no longer an umbilical
cord linking her to the safety of home but a dead instrument, to be discarded as quickly as possible because it
could not hide her any longer. There was a great crush as
the ship began its cumbersome maneuvering at the pier; the
passageways became crammed, filled, blocked with passengers, which turned out to be very foolish because they
stood for three quarters of an hour without moving.
Melissa found herself wedged among total strangers with
nothing to think about except the next few hours, but she
was so numbed from suspense that even this did not matter
greatly. Weakly she attempted to conjure up some kind of
reality from the immediate past but when she tried to recall
the faces of the college students, or the Fergusons, or even
Stearns, they proved too distant. She had seen none of
them for twenty-four hours; she was, again, alone—deserted by them all.

Fragments of conversation drifted past her:

*Very good trip, I thought.*

*Yes. A little more sun and it would have been perfect.*

*. . . They hushed it up, of course, shipping companies just don't approve of passengers dying aboard ship.*

*So that's what the commotion was! You know I saw them unloading what looked like a coffin at Cherbourg—I really did—and I thought, Why, that looks like a coffin if ever I saw one!*

*Yes, it happened a few hours before we reached Cherbourg. Poor devil was to have disembarked there.*

*Old man, I suppose . . .*

*No—quite young, the steward said. No more than forty. Suddenly fell to the floor in the corridor—made a terrible sound—and died at once. There'll be an autopsy, of course, there always is . . .*

*Traveling alone?*

*Yes, quite alone. Sad, isn't it?*

Abruptly murmurs of pleasure rose from the front of the line and with a surge the passengers began moving. "I don't like change," thought Melissa fretfully. "I liked this boat, I wanted to stay on it, I was just growing accustomed to it and now I have to start all over again, there isn't a single blasted thing I can hold on to, it's just move move move and nothing familiar at all." She wondered angrily why someone couldn't see what this was costing her and come to help her. Didn't anyone understand what this was like for her, did she really look so calm and knowledgeable and poised and self-sustaining?

The answer, of course, was that she did look all of these as she stood there in her blue cotton suit, hair brushed into silk, an aloof, amused smile on her lips. Only Dr. Szym would know because he would look behind the mask and into her eyes, which felt like deep funnels of terror and pleading.

"Ah, there you are!" shrilled Mrs. Comfort. "Come with us, Mrs. Aubrey!" The woman had planted herself firmly in Melissa's path, her three children surrounding her.

"Yes, but what are we to do?" asked Melissa ruefully.

"We go there," cried Mrs. Comfort, pointing to the glass-enclosed gangplank, "and we wait for our luggage, they call out our names over a loudspeaker when it arrives." She added peevishly, "I can't imagine where my husband is! That man is never around when he's needed."

On the ship Mrs. Comfort had been a bore to be avoided at all costs but now she wore the superiority of a woman who had gone through this countless times before. Melissa followed, and like sheep herded into a sorting house, they streamed over the gangplank into a huge terminal furnished with lines of tables and a scattering of chairs. Mrs. Comfort seized upon five of the chairs with triumph.

"Sit and hang onto your doll, Pamela. No, Herbert, no ice cream, sit and mind your little brother." To Melissa she said with exasperation, "It's so like a man to disappear when he's most needed." Her lips thinned. "Not enough—oh no—that we've got to uproot ourselves again so he can lecture for three months in Sweden, just look who has to wipe the noses, fetch the luggage, and at this rate go to Sweden and lecture for him if he doesn't show up."

"Perhaps he's inquiring what to do next."

Mrs. Comfort gave a roar of laughter. "Him? That'll be the day."

It occurred to Melissa that Mrs. Comfort had singled her out in expectation of complete accord on the subject of men, and she resented this conclusion about her singleness. Melissa also noted that although Mrs. Comfort gave no evidence of helplessness she had lost no time in securing a substitute prop for this traumatic moment of arrival. Mrs. Comfort might be a martyr but she did not travel alone, even if her husband was never around when he was needed, and Melissa felt a flare of anger at being so subtly used.

But Mrs. Comfort had not finished. "All very well for him to take the applause but who does the work, I ask you, and who wrestles with foreign schools and no hygiene at all, it'll be just like the last time, I know it. The stove won't work, the children will catch filthy diseases—and you just try to cook decent American food in Europe."

Melissa regarded her thoughtfully. "Surely it could be a wonderful experience living abroad?"

She had disappointed Mrs. Comfort. "Wonderful! Obviously men think so." Her eyes rested speculatively upon Melissa. "Men can be so thoughtless. Was it female trouble, dear?"

Startled, Melissa said, "I beg your pardon?"

"You said you were convalescing, you'd been in the hospital."

Melissa stood up, unable to bear the woman any longer. She said with distaste, "It wasn't quite the sort of hospital you're thinking of, Mrs. Comfort, nor quite that type of illness. It was a hospital for emotional disorders, and I'm recovering from a form of schizophrenia."

She had silenced the woman at last, and this brought a wonderful sense of achievement. "Now if you'll excuse me," she said with deadly politeness, "I'll leave and look for my suitcase." One glance at the open mouth and horrified eyes and Melissa found herself smiling as she walked away. *And to hell with you, Mrs. Comfort,* she thought, her anger giving her impetus. To the man at the desk she said crisply, "Now when will the luggage be arriving?"

He looked surprised. "It's downstairs, you can pick it up any time you want."

Melissa gave one triumphant glance at the hordes of people waiting passively for deliverance and she thought, "I asked!" All her life she had waited passively for such deliverances, as her parents had waited and then Charles, and now she tasted the heady sensation of action. It made her speculate about the Melissa that she would find waiting when all the false masks and the fears had been stripped from her. *Obviously aggressive,* she thought, relishing the idea, and she descended the stairs chuckling.

"Anything to declare?" asked the man in uniform, looming up in her path as she headed for the door.

Melissa glanced down at the suitcase she had retrieved from the counter. For the first time she remembered the package that Stearns had thrust upon her for delivery in

Majorca; she had almost completely forgotten about it, and
she had certainly not opened it yet to make sure it was a
book. She felt a surge of resentment toward Stearns. He
had been quite right to call it an imposition. "Two cartons
of cigarettes," she told the man.

He smiled at her. "Then welcome to Germany."

Melissa walked out into the sunlight to the waiting boat
train.

The compartment she chose was occupied by an old
man, and Melissa went in and stowed her suitcase away
and sat down. The man was asleep; he looked tired and
old. Melissa wished that she might sleep, too, for the train
was not to leave until it was filled. She leaned her head
against the cool windowpane and thought of the words she
had hurled at Mrs. Comfort, words that brought back memories she preferred to forget. But she had been unkind to
use Sunnybrook as a weapon of assault against the woman;
looking back she knew that when she reached Sunnybrook
it had been to emerge at last from an endlessly endured,
long, black tunnel. She had been blind until then, a mole
burrowing through layer after layer of darkness until patiently and slowly Dr. Szym had exposed her to precisely
measured gradations of light, and for the first time she saw
clearly. Saw herself. Saw Charles. Saw the world. But saw
herself most acutely of all, with the terrible intelligence of
insight.

Only then had come the terror with which she lived
now. It was as if Dr. Szym had taken her by the hand and
led her to the door of her tunnel and said, "There is the
sunlit garden waiting, the flowers and the blue sky. There
is your gift of freedom." But did no one realize that freedom was the most terrifying gift of all? Prisoners must feel
as she did when after years of captivity they faced their
liberation, for to live in darkness was to live in safety and
ease, without struggle, fear, doubt, or anxiety. Above all it
was to exist without change. Change frightened Melissa; it
frightened her so terribly that out of anguish she had em-
barked upon this trip, which she regarded as a form of

shock treatment. Deliberately she had set out to expose
herself to change after change, so that like a kaleidoscope
the shape of her life would be forced to fall into a different,
less rigid pattern.

The old man stirred and a snore escaped him. Melissa
brought her itinerary from her purse and unfolded it to read
again. The train would presently leave Bremerhaven and
an hour later arrive in Bremen; following a short wait it
would proceed to Hamburg, with arrival that evening at
nine and a reservation for the night at the Hotel Prem.
Tomorrow morning she would take the Alpen Express from
Hamburg to Copenhagen, arriving in Copenhagen in mid-
afternoon. On Saturday she would fly to Paris, and four
days later to Majorca. She tried to make it seem real to her
by going over and over it like a nun telling her beads.

But it did not seem real. The thought that tomorrow she
would be in Denmark was impossible to imagine when she
had not yet made her first stop in Germany. She decided to
take this one day by itself, to isolate this endless day of
disembarkation and attempt to make it familiar. She would
be spending the remainder of it on the train to Hamburg—
this was comforting to her, except that since it was already
late afternoon there arose the question of dinner: how was
she to manage food? She thought of leaving this compartment to ask if there was a dining car on the train; she
thought of leaving the train to buy crackers or chocolate,
but she was afraid, she felt tied to her seat by invisible
bonds she dared not sever. She was here, and because she
was here she was safe, but out there beyond the train lay
the terrors of insecurity. If she left she could imagine herself wandering farther and farther looking for the right person to ask, and then—horror of horrors—the train leaving
without her. The train was not supposed to leave yet, but
what if it did?

What if it did?

The thought of being left behind was intolerable. Her
only safety lay in following the rules of this printed itinerary without the slightest deviation: its instructions were a
path hacked out for her through a jungle of unpredictables,

but just one misstep, one error, and she would risk extinction. "I'm like a dinosaur," she thought wretchedly. "They were so damn rigid they couldn't adapt and just see what happened to them." It would be different if she had a companion; for others she could be daring, even reckless, but it was no joke to be alone. Alone she was afraid. No, it was better to sit very still and forget her own needs—except that to remain quiet was to think ahead to Hamburg. Nine o'clock was a terrible hour at which to arrive in a strange city, it would be late and dark and if the train was delayed would the hotel hold her reservation for her, or assume she wasn't coming? She dug out the itinerary again and was somewhat reassured to discover that a deposit had been made, and lacking this to concern her, felt her anxiety searching for a new outlet.

After a while the train began to move and Melissa took out her book and began to read, her interest divided between the printed words and the countryside sliding past her window.

But panic had been building inside of her all day, and it descended upon her in Hamburg as if it waited only for an object upon which to expel itself. The train was fifteen minutes late in arriving. Melissa was tired, hungry, nervous, and her suitcase heavy. She followed the crowds to the nearest exit but saw no taxis outside. She turned and plunged across the station to the opposite exit but there was no taxi stand there, either, and she felt old terrors of entrapment mount in her. To a passing woman she said, "Tak-see?" The woman smiled and pointed to the first exit that Melissa had abandoned, and Melissa picked up her bag and hurried back, almost insanely anxious now lest all the taxis had departed. It was late and it was nearly dark and she had become a child again belonging nowhere.

Still she found no taxi stand. It was like a nightmare.

She stopped and forced back her panic to stare around the huge vaulted station. There were large bright signs picturing Coca-Cola, summer holidays, toothpastes, and beautiful women; but there was simply no sign with a word approximating either taxi or exit, and she felt bereft, like an orphan. "I have lost a taxi," she thought forlornly, and wanly smiled at her absurdness. Why did she give in to these totally unreasonable, blind attacks of hysteria? "Calm down," she told herself. "Nobody's been lost forever in a railroad station." She put down her suitcase, took a deep breath and waited. Presently a man in naval uniform passed and she said, "Please—sprechen Sie English?"

"A little," he said.

"I can't find the taxis."

He smiled. "This way." He picked up her suitcase and returned her to the first exit. "Around there," he told her.

Melissa swore softly to herself. They had begun construction at this corner of the building and had erected a high rough fence on the left. She need only have walked a few more feet and peered beyond the fence to see the taxi stand. She was going to have to do much better than this.

"Thank you," she said. "Danke schön."

The man tipped his hat and walked away, and she reflected that he would never guess that he had soothed a child masquerading as a grown woman or performed, however briefly, the act of a parent for her. *Thank you for that, too,* she added fervently.

But the incident had taken its toll. When Melissa gained the privacy of her hotel room—which had, after all, been saved for her—she felt of no more solidity than a piece of paper. All content had been drained from her. When the bellhop left she stared at the door he closed behind him and longed to cry, but the tears that arose to her eyes were fraudulent, for only a real person could feel grief. Her glance swerved to the sumptuous hangings at the window, she moved to touch the ornate bureau and then she sat tentatively on the edge of the bed. These things at least were real but inside of her nothing felt real, for to be suspended between A and B was to be neither here nor there, and all sense of reality had been left behind her on the familiar, substantial boat. Her exacerbated nerves shrieked now for the comfort of one familiar face, a familiar language, a familiar place, she longed to give up and to rush home but this was Hamburg, Germany, and before she could reach home she must endure Copenhagen, Denmark, and then Paris, France, and then Palma, Majorca. It seemed endless, unendurable, she had the feeling that home was forever lost to her and that she could never return to it; it was the ultimate rejection and she must remain forever suspended between worlds, weightless, transparent, unreal.

Once Dr. Szym had said, "But we are all of us homeless from birth to death."

Tears flooded her eyes; how did people endure such homelessness? There was no one to whom she could turn, and no one who cared—not here, not anywhere; she had never felt so alone, so cut adrift from everything secure in her life. Yet tomorrow she must doggedly and relentlessly go on—she knew this, and wept at last for herself with great sobs of self-pity, for this was Hamburg, Germany—whatever that might be—and tomorrow, by another wearying, day-long process she would have to reach Copenhagen. Only by going on, by continuing, could she reach the end of this interminable odyssey. Ahead of her lay vast emptinesses of the unknown, holding terror after terror, but there was no escape, she could only weep and go on.

After a while, exhausted, she fell asleep.

# 3

THE COPENHAGEN HOTEL WAS MODERN AND LUXURIOUS, her room narrow but strikingly colorful with polished Danish woods and a vivid blue cover across her bed. With a hotel breakfast behind her Melissa lighted a cigarette and walked to the long window. She had arrived late yesterday afternoon after traveling by train and ferry, but she had not yet ventured out to experience her first European city; her moment of truth had arrived. There was no sun—somehow she had expected sun. There were three motor scooters parked under the trees that divided the avenue, and across the road a woman walked briskly, carrying a furled umbrella. This was Copenhagen, thought Melissa, and suddenly the immensity of it overwhelmed her: what was she to *do* with Copenhagen?

But she did not cry; she had done her crying in Hamburg, and now she was frozen, resolute, all tears spent. She thought, "I can't spend the next four days hiding in this room." She walked to the closet and brought out her raincoat and buckled it around her waist. She lifted her

suitcase to the bed, unlocked and unzipped it and removed
an umbrella. As she leaned over the suitcase she saw
Stearns' small white package lying exposed in a corner. It
seemed a long time ago that she had placed it there. Curious, she picked it up, studied it a moment, then broke the
string and tore open the paper.

It was indeed a book but it was a paperback that could
be bought anywhere, and this startled her. Its title was
*Basic Selections from Emerson: Essays Poems and Apo-
thegms*. Emerson—and it was not even a new book, she
noted, seeing both a crease and a smudge on its pasteboard
jacket. She turned to page 191 but it held no surprises, no
underscored words, no pencil notations along the margins,
it looked exactly like every other page. What was so valuable in this—was it a joke?

She shrugged. Crumpling up the white paper she threw
it into the wastebasket, and placed Stearns' book on the
bureau next to Robert Henri's *The Art Spirit*. Stearns had at
least contributed reading material for her evenings, and she
was reassured that his package did not contain contraband.
She replaced the suitcase and sat down with the abbre-
viated tourist map that she had been given upon register-
ing. The hotel was *here*, she discovered, circling it with a
pen, and although it looked some distance to the center of
Copenhagen, the Raadhuspladsen, she could reach it by
walking down the Ostergade, which was recommended as
Copenhagen's most exciting street of shops.

She tucked the map into her purse and stood up. It was
important to leave now, before she lost her courage, and
yet she could feel the weight of desire holding her back;
she did not want to go. But she was alone, she told herself
firmly and without self-pity, and she was to be alone for
the next two weeks: she must not expect magic rescues.
She wandered to the window again, wistfully hoping that
there might be sufficient life outside, observable through a
pane of glass, so that she might avoid or postpone leaving
the safety of this room. But nothing had changed and
standing there she reminded herself that everything in the
universe was as alone as she: each star shone by itself yet

was a part of the cosmos, each cloud racing across the sky was complete in itself yet moved with others in a same direction, each leaf on the tree outside her window remained a part of its tree. Separateness . . . it was a frightening word and one that had proven so unendurable that she had long ago forfeited her identity, her feelings, her emotions, even her integrity, so that she might lose the pain of its meaning. Now she had to go back in Time and recover what had been rejected: the lost emotions, unvalued opinions, scorned integrity.

"Oh, for heaven's sake, Melissa—GO," she said aloud, angrily.

She walked out, closing the door firmly behind her.

She was tired, and in the courtyard of the National Museum Melissa bought a soft drink from the vendor and carried it to a bench under the trees and sat down. The sun was mercifully shining now. In the far corner of her mind lurked the thought—she would not allow it entry—that it was only three o'clock in the afternoon and that ahead of her yawned the rest of a tourist's day and then a next and then another until dear God she would have to move on to another new city and again take a walk and visit a museum. This dread had the familiarity of an old friend waiting at her door, but she had learned from Dr. Szym that it was possible to select one's thoughts as well as one's friends. Coolly she lit a cigarette and coolly she took stock of both herself and her situation. She was, actually, doing a very good job with her day, but she admitted the temptation to return to the hotel now, carrying with her this sense of achievement to cherish for the rest of the day. It was as if she had gone just so far and must stop, saying to an invisible audience, "See how well I've done!" She was not sure who the audience was before whom she performed, but she suspected that, denied a touchable, physical presence she was performing now for God. There had to be someone, didn't there? It was all wrong—she knew this—it threw all her motives off-key, it ought to be herself for whom she made these efforts but the horrid truth was that she did not yet have enough of a self for whom to perform.

Yet something was consolidating within her, she could feel it: in Hamburg a fragile new toughness had been born out of her despair, and was deepening hour by hour. It was as if, denied contact with Dr. Szym, she had been forced to draw upon untapped reserves inside of her. To return now to her hotel at this hour would be a giving up—she saw this clearly—for if she returned at three o'clock today then she might return at two tomorrow, and at one the next day, and not go out at all the following day. No, it was very necessary for her to keep going, mindlessly and mechanically perhaps, but to keep going.

She drew on her cigarette and looked back upon the last few hours: she had visited the Carlsberg Glyptopek, lunched just inside Tivoli Garden at the Konditori, and a few moments ago had completed a tour of the National Museum. Enthralled by the Islamic costumes in the museum, she had even brought out her sketchbook and colored pencils to jot down their patterns and marvelous colors—one would almost have believed her to be normal. At the Glyptopek the early Gauguins had struck her as being interesting but entirely disillusioning, and she was pleased to have reached such a conclusion because it was an opinion. She had enjoyed her day so far in a surprisingly contented—if self-conscious—way. She knew that if she were with Charles he would be checking off ten museums on a list and urging her joylessly and dutifully toward an eleventh: she was therefore becoming aware that traveling alone could have advantages, and this too was a conclusion entirely her own. Considering the satisfaction that lay in having collected two opinions, she pushed out her feet and happily wriggled her toes. Yes there just might be compensations in traveling alone if she looked upon the more comfortable, even voluptuously comfortable, aspects of freedom. If she could be enough to herself.

She decided to try it for a little longer, and to encourage this new resistance to ease, and at the same time rest her tired feet, she would risk the four o'clock bus tour of Copenhagen. It had the advantage of being a happy compromise because nothing would be demanded of her except that she sit on a bus and be guided about the city; there was no possible chance of her becoming lost, and it would keep her occupied until six, after which she would have earned the right to feel absolutely safe with a quiet dinner in the hotel's dining room, a long hot bath, and reading in bed.

She jumped to her feet and with real zest strode across the square to the office of the tour company to buy a ticket. "The bus sits there," said the young man, pointing toward the plaza.

"Tak!" she cried gaily, and for the first time felt gay, in command of her life and capable of making decisions. She climbed into the nearly empty bus and chose a seat in the center, next to the window. As she seated herself she opened her purse to extract cigarettes and to her chagrin ores and kroners fell out and rolled across the floor. "Oh dear," she gasped.

"You," said the young woman across the aisle, "are American."

Melissa glanced up and smiled. "You too?"

"You need some help." She leaned from her seat and gathered up a few coins for Melissa. "I'm from Los Angeles."

"Massachusetts," said Melissa, on her knees. The girl wore slacks and a fur coat, her honey-colored hair was long and unkempt, and she spoke with the affected drawl of an Eastern finishing school but she spoke English, and she was alone. "For how long are you traveling?"

"The summer," the girl said in a beautifully throaty, rueful voice. "And you?"

"Three weeks. Are you traveling alone or with your family?"

"Good God, alone. Is there any other way?"

Melissa winced at this remark, and dropping the last of the coins into her purse returned to her own seat beside the window. "What countries have you been visiting?"

A man walked up the aisle, glanced at the vacant seat beside the Californian and then at the vacant seat beside Melissa, and chose the latter. It placed a wall between her and the girl, and with a feeling of acute dislike toward the man Melissa had to lean forward to hear the girl's reply. "Spain, and then Portugal, and I just flew in from Paris."

Melissa nodded. "I go to Paris next, and then to Majorca. How did you find Spain?"

"Dirty, of course," replied the girl, "but I had friends there who took me to Granada. It's utterly out of this world. Compelling. Marvelous." She pronounced it *mahvlas*.

It was tiring to lean forward. Melissa smiled and sank back. The man beside her said, "You will enjoy Majorca, you know. It's beautiful beyond description." He had the clipped accent of an Englishman.

She stiffened. She had thought his manners abominable when he inserted himself between her and the girl across the aisle; now it seemed that he eavesdropped as well. The new Melissa, heady with opinions and conclusions, turned cold with disdain. "You've been there then," she said with such indifference that her words could almost have been yawned at him.

"Yes, a few years ago." He seemed oblivious of her rejection; he brought a pack of cigarettes from his jacket and before removing one for himself held out the packet to her. The gesture was an assumption of intimacy that affronted Melissa. Intimacy was always a threat that sent her into flight. "No, thank you," she said scornfully, but in the act of refusing she looked into the man's face and it surprised her enough to weaken her defenses, which always doubled at signs of aggression. He appeared pleasant, relaxed, friendly, even distinguished, with a look of inborn fastidiousness. She noted a square face and jaw and a pair of expressive black eyebrows. His hair was thick and liberally salted with gray. No devil's horns at all, she told herself dryly and felt suddenly narrow-minded and provincial.

"Have you been long in Copenhagen?" he asked.

She said politely, "Since late yesterday afternoon. And you?"

"I flew in this morning from Berlin."

"You must have seen the Wall then."

He nodded. "Extremely depressing. I shouldn't have liked to miss it but I was quite happy to leave."

The driver of the tour bus climbed into his seat and a young woman in uniform followed and began testing the small hand microphone. "It looks as if we're about to leave," her companion said.

"Yes, it does." To fill the interval she gave him her last polite question, for she had been traveling long enough to understand that very few people went beyond the amenities of *where have you been* and *for how long are you traveling.* "And for how long are you traveling?" she asked.

He crossed his legs comfortably and drew on his cigarette, allowing the smoke to stream from his nostrils. "I'm traveling around the world," he said. "A six-month tour which is nearing its end now. I shall be at home by late August."

"Six months," she echoed. It was a surprisingly long time, and a dozen questions rose in her. Curiosity won and she said, "But how could you arrange to be away for so long, and have you grown tired of traveling? Did you plan the trip for yourself or are you with an organized tour?"

He smiled. "Oh, quite alone. Yes, I grow jaded at times but never for long. I inherited a little money last year and decided to do something very important to me, and so I asked for a sabbatical. I'm an archaeologist, you see, and—"

"Archaeologist!" she repeated warmly. "But I once fully intended to become one, I really did—I was all of thirteen at the time," she added humorously. "Except I turned to art instead."

He glanced at her quickly. "Did you really! What sort of art?"

"Painting primarily—I'm a painter." Even this had lost its meaning for her but saying it aloud to this man made it seem real again.

"Professional?"

"I have been in the past," she said. "Several New York gallery exhibits among others—but not lately," she added honestly. "Nothing lately." Vividly she recalled Charles' growing irritation over her work: *you used to paint such gay, charming, childlike pictures,* he would say, *but now they're gloomy, dark, with just one lonely figure, you're not like that, I don't like it.* Her lips curved ironically as she remembered.

"Then you must be very talented," the man said, regarding her with appreciation.

"Good afternoon, ladies and gentlemen," said the bright young tour guide, smiling at them. "Today we are taking you on a land and water tour of Copenhagen, in which you will see, among other things . . ."

"Do you dig up corbeled vaults and disc barrows?" she asked impulsively, the words coming back to her from long ago, "or do you work in a museum?"

"You really do know something about it," he said, giving her a quizzical glance. "Actually you might say that art is my line, too, but ancient pre-historic art rather than historical. Yes, I work in a museum but I frequently go off to the excavations when I feel stale."

"The digs," said Melissa, smiling.

"Yes." He smiled, too.

"You're English, aren't you?"

"Yes, but I live in Greece at present. It feels quite comfortable—I was born there—and it's where I shall return in August. You of course are American. For how long are you traveling?"

"Only three weeks."

"Alone?"

She nodded. "Yes."

"I am surprised. Do you find it lonely?"

Melissa hesitated, then firmly turned her back on yesterday. She said instead, shyly, "Of course I'm only two days off the ship but I was just thinking as I boarded the bus how free I feel quite suddenly. Free to go exactly where I choose to go and not where someone else wants me to go. To please them." It was a declaration of independence hurled at the world, it was an acknowledgment of her realization that she need no longer perpetuate the child image that Charles had insisted upon until its weight nearly destroyed her.

He had finished his cigarette; he brought out another and this time she accepted one. "But don't you," he said thoughtfully, "don't you at times miss there being someone with whom to share the beautiful moments?"

She gave him a startled glance. She had lived so long among people who could not feel life that his words caught her unaware. Beauty was a word very private to her, its meaning something she was accustomed to containing within herself; yet this man brought out the word as he might draw a pebble from his pocket to finger, to reflect upon and acknowledge. "Yes, that can be true," she said very softly. "I've felt that." She realized she was almost whispering.

"There was a moment in Hong Kong that literally took my breath away," he said. "A sunset impossible to describe without leaning on clichés. I don't carry a camera—"

"Nor do I," she said with surprise. "It seemed more important to see if I could carry away all of this *inside* of me—"

He turned and looked at her with pleasure. "But exactly! That was precisely my feeling, too."

The tour guide continued to smile and explain to them what they were seeing of Copenhagen but neither the man nor Melissa were listening; they were making discoveries of their own. She liked him, she could talk to him, and conversation flowed between them with ease. Vividly Melissa recalled the dozens of people with whom she had made arduous conversation since her trip began, she remembered the underlying sense of loneliness, of frustration and confinement that she had felt in talking with them. It was missing now. Why, wondered Melissa; what different, more magical ingredients were brought to this conversation? There were truly no similarities between them in either background or experience, it had to be a thing of the spirit, it was the only explanation she could find.

He said suddenly, "You know, before this tour I bought a ticket to the evening's performance at Tivoli Garden, which happens to be a singer of whom I'm quite fond. I'm sure I can exchange my single for two if you'd care to join me."

"But I'd enjoy that very much," she told him honestly.

"Good!"

Where had her shyness gone? She was accustomed to feeling it hug her like a cloak and instead she felt light, buoyant, free. Only an hour ago she had decided that she could manage life alone and presto! this man had appeared out of nowhere. Perhaps renunciation was the magic formula, she thought with a faint smile; and woven into this thought like a glittering thread was the supposition that a man who traveled for six months alone could surely not be married. Was *this* to be her reward at last for the suffering of the past months, and for this heroic attempt to fight her way back to life?

When the bus returned to the Raadhuspladsen, where the tour had begun, they had just reached the subject of psychiatry: Melissa had quoted something of Dr. Szym's and had identified him as her psychiatrist; it was the first reference to any personal life that had entered their conversation. Helping her descend from the bus he said, "We don't have many psychiatrists in Greece, you know. It's quite a different world there. It interests me, your having visited one. I hope you'll tell me about it." They paused on the sidewalk. "You said you'd like to change before we dine. In which direction is your hotel?"

Indeed, Melissa had announced, with an assertiveness quite new to her, that she would like to change before dinner. "Up that street," she said, and leaning over his map she punctured with a fingernail the location of her hotel.

"But that's very near mine," he said. "We can take this tram that's coming."

Tram—she enjoyed the phrases he used which emphasized his accent. He grasped her hand and they raced toward the trolley to climb aboard. As she sat down, Melissa considered the direction in which their conversation was heading: she looked ahead to the barrier called Sunnybrook and considered it judiciously. It had been all very well to hurl it like an epithet at Mrs. Comfort but this man was not Mrs. Comfort and she did not want either to alarm or bore him. If Sunnybrook had ended six months ago she would leave it there, rooted in the past.

"What took you to a psychiatrist?" he was asking, with no alarm at all.

"Depression," she told him. "I grew very depressed over a period of two years."

"Interesting. I assume you mean something far deeper than the depressions we all feel now and then."

"Oh yes. I looked the word up in the dictionary once," she confided. "I was surprised to find that it means to degrade or to pull down. It felt just like that: a terrible weight."

"But what caused it?"

She laughed at him. "You ask—just like that—when it's taken a year of visits and hundreds of dollars to find out. But in capsule form it came from a fear of being myself, and therefore from too many wrong turnings in my life."

"To thine own self you weren't true," he said.

"Exactly." As they jumped off the tram she thought how quick he was at grasping concepts and she told him so. "Has traveling alone for six months sharpened your perceptions or are you always this way?"

He said seriously, "Actually I haven't been alone for the entire six months, my wife traveled with me for the first five weeks and then returned to Greece."

His wife . . . Not by a flicker of an eyelash did she show her terrible disappointment, her reaction to this shattering interruption of a dream. Was nothing to be as she hoped, she wondered; was reality nothing but adjustment to one disillusionment after another? For just one second she allowed bitterness to enter, noted cynically the calculated timing of this man's announcement, when she was already committed to an evening with him; and then, recovering, acknowledged the fact that he need not have mentioned a wife at all. But was there to be no one at all to rescue her from her aloneness? A wave of anger passed over her, directed entirely at Charles, her husband, for inadvertently thrusting her into this harsh, cold world that had not, after all, been waiting for her to wake up, nor was standing by now to reward her for her awakening.

Both bitterness and anger passed. What was it Dr. Szym had said so many times? "Life isn't easy." But why wasn't life easy, she wondered despairingly. It had been made easy for her as a child and she had always assumed its ease as an adult. Painting had come easily to her, and with rewards; why couldn't life?

She did not comment on his having a wife. She had lately watched far older dreams disintegrate, and with only one last and poignant farewell to what might have been, she adjusted to what was. She was enjoying this man; she would, for the first time in her life, accept her enjoyment of him as an adult, without trying to manipulate or to cling. Why not? She would never see him again, and she had certainly never before met anyone like him. Only children tore up gifts that did not totally please them.

He had continued talking, and she had not heard him. Now he said, "This looks like your hotel—yes, there's the sign. Mine is only two blocks away. Shall we meet for a drink in an hour?"

She suddenly laughed. "I don't even know your name!"

He looked chagrined. "Good heavens!" They smiled at each other and he said, delighted, "But this has never happened to me before, it proves how very unimportant names are, doesn't it? We have talked like this for how long—nearly three hours?—and know each other without any introduction at all. My name is Adam Burrill."

"And mine is Melissa Aubrey."

"Melissa—I like that."

"And how do you come to be traveling alone?" he asked an hour later. They were seated in the bar of her hotel with drinks and cigarettes.

She could speak of Charles now. "My marriage has come to an end," she said. "You might say as an outcome of therapy. Yes, I guess you really could say that," she added, surprised by the thought. "Psychiatry really did destroy it. I had to leave."

"Because therapy changed you," he mused.

She nodded. "Yes. And he couldn't change, which was the nature of his disease." She said reflectively, "Change frightens people, you know. It frightens *me*, but Charles— Charles can't admit change of any kind into his life. It's what came near to destroying me, the changeless life we led. Then when I began to change I became a threat to him and he went nearly wild. I had to leave—really—for survival."

"Survival of the spirit." He nodded.

Again he pleased and surprised her; she had known only literal, material people. "Yes."

"Then you are braver than he. Braver than most of us. You are doing what a great many people would like to do but can't."

"Not brave," she said, shaking her head. "I only remember what it was like to be—" She almost said ill. "What it was like to be buried alive." For it was surprisingly ironic: her need to avoid aloneness had driven her to Charles, who was so detached from life that he had made her ill enough to be cured.

"What sort of man is this Charles of yours?" he asked, lighting her a fresh cigarette and leaning forward with real interest.

She frowned. "He's intelligent—or started out to be. It's just that he stopped changing—that word again! I think he collected all of his opinions and beliefs and outlooks before he turned twenty-one; he put them into a satchel and said, 'There, that's done' with a feeling of enormous relief, and for Charles that was that. He was totally formed."

Adam nodded. "Yes, that makes a picture."

"It has terrible ramifications, of course. There's no curiosity—it's dangerous, it might open one to change. It sadly limits your friends, too: they mustn't ever be curious, or controversial or stimulating or intellectual because they'd become a threat then, your opinions would be chal-

lenged and certainly wouldn't seem so profound. A feeling
of superiority has to be maintained at any cost—for pro-
tection—and this pretty much limits and strangles every
relationship. There's such maneuvering, you see, to remain
admired and looked up to and unchallenged. Above all
there has to be a distance kept between you and other
human beings so that you'll never be exposed." She
shrugged. "And with distance how can there be intimacy?
It is impossible."

Adam shook his head. "It's difficult to imagine your
life. No parties, I suppose."

She was shocked. "Good heavens no."

"None at all?"

She shook her head. "Charles didn't approve of people
drinking." She suddenly burst out laughing. "I've just remembered: he complained that what he disliked about
drinking was that it changed people."

"Good heavens, even there," said Adam incredulously.
"But you have lived a very grim sort of life then. Why on
earth did you marry him?"

She smiled ruefully. "What Charles conceals is his fear
of life, and—well, I too am afraid of life."

He leaned back. "It's honest of you to admit."

"One learns honesty in therapy." She said with a sigh, "I
suppose I kept hoping he would rescue me from my own
fears, that he would help me. What I didn't understand is
that when we marry it's usually our subconscious that
chooses for us. Charles appeared very full of life—he
gives that illusion because he is in constant motion—but
his incessant motion only conceals the fact that actually his
life goes nowhere. I think my subconscious must have
shouted, 'Hooray, the perfect man, marry him and you will
always be safe from life because Charles is ten times more
afraid than you and this will protect you.'" She smiled
faintly. "Now at last I understand what happened to me and
I pick up the pieces. Except after so many years of atrophy
—of no visible signs of life—it's like never having lived
before, like not knowing the rules, not knowing quite
what's—well, real."

"But still—better?"

She said fervently, "It will have to be, it must be. I can't be like Charles. He lived—how shall I explain it?—in a tightly circumscribed circle of lilliputian dimensions. To step outside of that rigid circle was to experience terrible anxiety and insecurity." She hesitated. "I have to expose myself now, quite ruthlessly, to those insecurities. Like an inoculation."

There was silence and then Adam reached out his hand and covered hers with his. "I'm glad I've met you, Melissa Aubrey," he said.

They reached Tivoli at dusk, and entering its gates walked down a winding path toward the heart of the gardens. "This is a magic place, I feel it," he said, and reached for her hand and grasped it.

She smiled, touched by his sharing gesture and only a little frightened by it.

"Let's dine here," he said, pointing to a structure of glass and timber. "I'll order some very good wines for you to end your years of deprivation."

"Just now they feel like centuries of deprivation," she told him happily.

"A table for two," he told the maître d', and to Melissa, "Have you ever had wienerschnitzel?"

"Never."

"Then you really must try it." For the next few moments he conferred gravely with both a wine steward and a waiter while Melissa watched with a mixture of amusement and curiosity. Then they were alone again, and with ease the old conversation resumed. "What you've said about your marriage interests me," he said, leaning back in his chair. "I don't love my wife but I would say that we have a good marriage. We live quite separate lives—very stimulating ones for each of us—and see very little of one another but when we meet we have things to talk about."

"That sounds—just a little cynical," she told him, frowning over it.

He shrugged. "What, after all, is a good marriage? I

don't know of any, really. I sometimes think it is a matter of remaining out of one another's way."

"Now that really is cynical," she said, laughing.

He seemed not to hear. "What we talk about is of course quite superficial but—at least we talk. In a good many marriages there is not even that."

She nodded. "Yes. Two people sitting at a table. Watching others. Nothing to say."

"I've had affairs," he went on soberly. "A number of them. I'm sure my wife has had them, too. It becomes a pattern, a way of life."

She struggled with this concept of marriage. "But aren't you afraid—that is, isn't there the danger of—I may sound naïve but what if you should fall deeply in love with one of your women?"

He smiled sadly. "Oh yes, I'm vulnerable. It's a hazard, it's a very real risk. But it's never happened. I don't want to leave my wife, you know. If I should, for instance, have an affair with you—I use this only as an example, you understand—I would take from you your warmth, cherishing it, and then go on."

She said dryly, "Do you make a public announcement of this each time?"

"I'm always honest. I try to be."

She shook her head. "I think it's extremely artful. Don't you think it's rather like waving a red flag in front of a woman?"

He looked puzzled. "How do you mean?"

She smiled. "I mean it's very clever of you. I'm sure each woman pays no attention at all to what you say, knowing deep down in her bones that she will be the one to make you lose both your head and your wife. She sets out to prove that you're attainable."

He said ruefully, "You have a dismaying knack for making me feel like a cad."

"But you *are* one," she told him, laughing. "I've read of your sort in books."

"I cannot impress you at all," he said with mock helplessness.

"No, you can't. That's the native good sense in me speaking. I do have some, you know, deep down under all my silly problems. Someone like you would be very dangerous to me." She laughed. "Good heavens—extremely!"

"Dangerous? How?"

She stopped laughing, for really it was no joke at all. "Because you would hurt me."

"But I would never hurt you."

She hesitated. "Yes," she thought soberly, "you would inflict the greatest hurt of all, for you would fly away and leave me." And that, she realized, stated her problem very succinctly: that only an unchanging permanence had ever felt safe for her. In a world of flux, of arrivals and departures, she was totally lost, for there was then nothing to hang on to, there were no Absolutes, no guarantees that she mattered. She could not tolerate the anxiety of anything that she might lose. Lacking all certainty within herself she must find it spuriously in other people, seizing and clutching at them until she had bound them to her and placed them in neat rows of coffins, where they were owned, accessible, lifeless—but safe.

Aloud she said only, "I could be hurt because I have never really loved, either."

He looked at her searchingly. "Then yes," he said softly, "you are vulnerable, too. Extremely so."

It was an unexpected moment. She stared at him, unable to speak; he had looked inside of her, he had seen. She felt in his words an acknowledgment of herself as a person and was strangely moved by it. Only Dr. Szym had ever looked within her; no one else. *Yes, you are vulnerable, too.* The compassion of it brought tears to her eyes and she had to look down and pretend to be busy with her demitasse. At last, very lightly, she said, "It must be shockingly late."

He glanced at his watch and smiled. "So late that it is now intermission time. Shall we try for the second half?"

"Why not?"

"I feel I've not talked so much in years." He gestured to the waiter, paid the bill and they left.

Outside it had grown dark, turning Tivoli Garden into a

land of enchantment. Lights bloomed everywhere like flowers: filigreed lanterns, round globes of pale gold and white and pink, discs of blue and deep violet, lights and shapes of such whimsy and delight as Melissa had never seen before. "Oh, look—Adam, look," she gasped, stopping. Ahead of them, framed against the dark sky, stood a huge, ancient oak tree dressed with an embroidery of twinkling stars: not a Christmas tree but a fairyland tree. Clusters of tiny white lights had been hung at intervals all through the tree's branches, and as the night wind filled the leaves it set every star to dancing. "But it's unbelievable," she whispered, feeling the beauty of it clutch at her heart, and as she gazed, filling her eyes with it, beauty rooted her to this moment in Time as securely as this tree had rooted itself in centuries of earth.

The moment passed, and she became herself again, mortal, yet not quite the same because she had been moved and touched by beauty.

When they emerged from the theater the lights were slowly being extinguished in the park. It was already the morning of another day and Melissa sighed with the realization that it was ending, it was over. "My tree is dark," she said, pointing to the huge tree empty now of lights.

"The Danes know how to live," he mused, looking up into the mysterious dark foliage of the tree.

Dreamily she said, "That's a rash statement, you know, they have a rather high suicide rate."

"Do they really! I wonder why."

"Actually I can tell you," she said with a smile in her voice. "I told you that I have spent my life reading, not living, and before I left home I came across something about the Danes. It seems that as a race they have the same problems I have."

"Really?"

"Mmm. Very strong dependency needs, with suicidal tendencies when their dependencies vanish. It's the way they're punished as children. With guilt."

"But aren't most of us punished in that way?" he mused.

"Yes, but there's a double bind involved. They're denied any outlet for hostility after they've been made to feel the guilt. It was pointed out, for instance, how different their fairy tales are from those of other European countries. Other fairy tales have evil and terror and wicked witches in them but not the Danish stories, they're all sweetness and forgiveness and a giving up for others. So aggressiveness is repressed, they're unable to acknowledge their frustration, and they grow up crooked."

"To build beautiful gardens like this which are the very antithesis of evil and doubt."

She thought, "Oh if only I'd been able to talk like this to Charles!" She laughed suddenly. "But perhaps it's better just to admire a fairyland and not look behind the façade. I do like Tivoli."

"And so do I," he said. "Now what shall we do tomorrow?"

His words caught her unaware and she felt a quickening of warmth. So this was to go on . . . She realized that for the first time in her life it had not occurred to her whether she was to see this man again. She had become totally absorbed in each moment, savoring every nuance and odd turning that it took, being completely herself without pretense or maneuvering or guile. And now it was to go on . . .

"The tourist book has a long list," she said quickly, to conceal her pleasure. "The Changing of the Guard at the Palace, the Tuborg beer factory, et cetera, et cetera."

"The et ceteras sound especially interesting," he said with a smile. "Suppose we meet at ten outside your hotel." They entered the lobby, quiet and dim at this hour. He stopped at the bottom of the staircase and released her hand. "Until ten," he said, and kissed her lightly on the lips. "Shall we continue these soul-searchings tomorrow?"

"Agreed," she said, smiling at him. "Until ten then." With the dignity of someone who feels of infinite value she ascended the stairs but at the landing she stopped, a sense of wonder spreading through her, for she had just recalled

the Melissa who sat in a museum park and promised herself the safety of a quiet evening, a long bath, and a new
book. Delight filled her, and standing there alone on the
landing thousands of miles from home, Melissa threw back
her head and laughed with joy.

# 4

They met at ten o'clock, softly, eagerly. Was it time or sleep that had changed them, wondered Melissa, and she decided, being new to life, that relationships of any value must grow even during hours of separation to make the next encounter so astonishing. She saw Adam walking toward her and felt not only anticipation but a sense of familiarity such as she would feel toward someone known for a very long time. And her anticipation was keen: she was aware that yesterday had been only an introduction, a clearing-away of detail; for if a friendship or an intimacy was, like therapy, a matter of layers—and both therapy and friendship possessed the common denominator of discovering a self—then only the outermost layers had been peeled away yesterday, with more to come today.

In turn she survived Adam's curious and searching glance. Coming to a stop before him she said, "Good morning!"

He neither smiled nor spoke but tucked her arm under his in unspoken acknowledgment, and they began to walk toward the Bredgade. "You've breakfasted?" he asked at last.

"Sumptuously."

"Good. I propose that we have a late lunch at that very charming outdoor restaurant in Tivoli Garden, the one beside the lake with the swans. In the meantime, what shall we do with this bright, charming morning?"

They caught a tram to the State Museum and spent the next hours exploring its art treasures, except that for Melissa it was more of an experience than a tour because of Adam's encyclopedic knowledge of art. Nothing had escaped his interested eye, his taste was catholic and unlimited, and despite a moderately adequate training, Melissa was overwhelmed by the gaps in her knowledge and reduced to the status of a student. They talked, discussed, and argued—"how dare you know so much?" she demanded hotly; "But I am the complete dilettante," he replied, "I know all and create nothing"—until at last, drained but satisfied, they walked out into the sunlight.

"I'm exhausted," she told him, smiling.

"Gallery feet," he said, nodding. "But if you can endure a little more of the dog that bit you I think we may soon sit down. I see trees over there, and benches."

"Botanik Häve," read Melissa helpfully from a sign.

He consulted his map. "Botannical Gardens. Not much farther, can you make it?"

"I could wish for a St. Bernard with a flask," she admitted.

"We should have brought our own. Art galleries are notoriously dry."

They reached a bench and sat down, and Adam lit cigarettes for them. "Bliss," she murmured ecstatically.

"Absolute," he agreed. "It's always a relative thing, is it not?"

"Mmm."

He turned his head and looked at her appreciatively. "You are extremely good company."

"Always," she teased, smiling.

"You're made up of such contradictory bits and pieces

—naïve and yet not at all naïve. I believe I could make a real sophisticate of you in three months' time."

"With a diploma and badge saying 'true sophisticate'?"

"At least."

He grasped her hand and they sat contentedly in the warm sun without speaking until Adam said suddenly, "Happy?"

She nodded. "Yes. Yes, I'm thinking that it's almost worth growing up crooked to arrive at this moment when I sit in the sun in Copenhagen, Denmark, and wriggle my toes."

"Peculiar expression, crooked."

"One I've always used—always."

"You've told me where it's taken you but what causes this—crookedness, as you put it?"

"Why, love of course," she said flippantly. She turned her head to stare across the park for this was a difficult matter to speak about. "I'm sorry," she said quickly. "That doesn't answer your question, does it, because what is love? But I read in a textbook last year about how they investigated six women who'd been rejected as children. They tried to discover the difference in them, you know? What made some all right and others—well, like me."

"Yes?"

"It's funny. The mothers who said to their children. 'I loathe you, get out of my sight' or 'You've been in my way ever since you were born, you brat'—the funny thing is, these girls were the healthier ones."

She had startled him. "*They* were?"

She nodded. "Yes. Because as children they knew where they stood. They knew they were rejected, disliked, not wanted. They knew, and it freed them to find substitutes, their knowing gave them a sense of reality. It was the others—the mothers with dripping sweet voices and devouring arms—" Her voice trembled and when she resumed it was cold, impersonal. "*They* covered up their hatred and resentment. They would say 'I love you, now go away.' And the child would feel the dislike, yet it was cloaked in the name of love and the child grew bewildered and full of despair. How can a child come to grips with hostility that's masked as love? It gives the child nothing solid in his life to grow against, and it's unendurable and so after a while the bewildered child begins to just give up. He or she withdraws from life. From entanglements."

"Withdraws," he mused. "You paint a terrifying picture. But you scarcely seem withdrawn, you know, you appear very outgoing and just see where you are, you're sitting in a park in Copenhagen, Denmark."

She looked at him and said softly, "It happens inside, Adam. Inside of me there are four barbed wire fences around my heart and at the very center a brick wall. I'm afraid of closeness, of feeling."

"Of feeling . . ." He frowned.

She hesitated. "Even of expressing it," she admitted. "I remember there was a patient of Dr. Szym's I used to talk with over a period of weeks. At first it was 'how are you' and then, very shyly, we exchanged news of our progress. One day as he was leaving the office he suddenly and impulsively reached out a hand and touched my arm. As a gesture of—well, of warmth, of thanks." She shook her head. "Inside of me I jumped, I really did. That one small gesture—it alarmed me."

"Like an invasion?"

She nodded eagerly. "Yes, you do see it, don't you. That's why I jumped. And yet I was so warmed by it really, I felt so touched by the gesture I wanted to cry. It meant he liked me. I want life, you know, we all want life even when we're conditioned against it."

"How repeatedly you must have been hurt once to react that way," he said soberly.

"You'll have me crying, Adam, really you will. Talking to you is like talking to Dr. Szym except that you sympathize." She jumped to her feet to end a conversation that had touched deep chords inside of her.

Adam was smiling. "And psychiatrists don't sympathize?"

"Well—they sympathize with the suffering but not with the cause, if you know what I mean. I mean, they know very well that their patients have spent years feeling sorry for themselves so why perpetuate it? They don't say 'oh you poor thing,' they say 'all right, that happened, but what are you going to do about it?' They treat patients as adults—or as potential adults," she said with a wry smile, "which is flattering, too, but it's terribly nice to be sympathized with. As an equal. As a fellow human."

"As a fellow traveler," he said with a twinkle. "Do sit down, where are you going?"

She sat down. "In my country the expression 'fellow traveler' has disagreeable implications, you know. I hoped we were going to have some lunch. You know, we really must visit that Tuborg beer factory," she added sternly.

"Yes, and the palace—"

"And rent a bicycle—"

"And that sailboat—"

"They'll ask what you saw in Copenhagen," she teased.

He laughed. "Good God, what on earth shall I tell them? I'd have to say I behaved like a schoolboy, wandering the streets with a girl. I never walk at home; if I have an errand half a block away, I drive."

"I know," she said delightedly.

"And here I am sitting in a park holding your hand and resting two very tired feet. I haven't visited a nightclub—"

"—and of course they'll ask about the famous Danish blondes—"

"And instead I am with a very charming American, but in Copenhagen of all places."

"No sense at all," she agreed.

"And a very thirsty and demanding American at that." He leaned over and slipped on his shoes. "I've never been accused of a lack of gallantry. How far is that restaurant in Tivoli, do you think?"

"Miles. Simply miles."

"Good God. Well—ready?" he asked, rising.

"At last yes," she said.

He held out his arms so that she walked into them and he held her for a moment, gently. "You have the uncanniest knack for looking fresh and rested," he said.

"That's my unlived life," she reminded him.

He lifted her chin and gravely looked into her eyes. "And I have lived too well and too much, and forgotten all the simple pleasures of life. Thank you for this." He kissed her lightly on the mouth and they began walking arm in arm down the path.

"So I make you feel young then?" she asked flippantly, to cover the treacherous feeling of closeness she had survived.

"Not young. Alive again." He hesitated. "I'm not a particularly good person. I have crowded more into my life than most men but at times I have been, oh quite ruthless—"

"With women," she said, nodding gravely.

"Yes." He stopped and gave her a faint smile. "How do you know that?"

She wanted to say, "Because I know you," but she was afraid of frightening him. It seemed inconceivable to her that she already knew him better, in the space of a day, than she had known Charles during their years of marriage. But she only returned his smile and shook her head.

"One drifts into things carelessly, with hopes that are never realized, and—"

"I know," she said.

"As it is, I have lived a full life—a sensuous, enjoyable, and quite splendid life—but not a particularly worthwhile one. The lines I see in my mirror each morning are lines of dissipation, I know this. I truly envy you beginning your life again, a second chance, a new change."

"I hope I don't muff it," she said wistfully.

He stopped and looked at her. "Don't, Melissa. We're counting on you not to—all of us."

"All?" She was amused.

"The ones who are denied it. The ones who have lost too much innocence to begin again."

"Or too much hope," she said quietly, feeling the sadness that ran through this man like a thread. "You know," she said, and stopped, smiling.

"Go ahead. Say it."

She laughed. "I'm not the sort of person you'd know at home. Not at all. I'm not beautiful and I'm not sophisticated and yet—is it because of this or because we'll never see each other again that we can talk like this?"

"Does it matter? Isn't it simply—enough?"

She considered this a moment. "Yes—yes, it is enough," she said, and realized that this was true. "I'm grateful, Adam."

He nodded. "One must always be grateful."

"Are you a fatalist?"

He smiled. "I know that I very nearly didn't take that four o'clock tour of Copenhagen yesterday—and yet I did."

She thought, "Yes and out of all the days in which either of us might have come to Copenhagen, out of all the dates blindly, casually chosen months ago for an arrival in this city, we entered that bus on the same day and at the same hour from points at opposite ends of the world. Could it be possible," she wondered wistfully, "that somewhere out there—cutting through all the meaningless chaos—a Being or a Force had leaned over this crazy globe to give one very small Melissa Aubrey a gift of value to help her on . . ?"

They sat on benches just above the water, the sun on their faces and a table between them. The sounds of water lapping against the piles held a drowsy, nostalgic note for Melissa, reminding her of long sunny Cape Cod afternoons as a child. A family of swans drifted on the pond below them, formal, elegant, and proud. Occasionally someone from the surrounding tables would walk to the railing and throw crumbs to the swans and they would dip their long necks graciously and with a touch of condescension.

"Drink your beer," said Adam.

"I'm so busy looking," she told him happily. She was remembering her first hours in Copenhagen when alone she had walked the streets and looked at the people in the outdoor cafés, and she had wondered then if she would one day have the courage to walk in among them and sit at a

table. And it had seemed to her—was it only yesterday?—
the story of so many lost years: Melissa walking past life
and looking, always looking, always longing to enter the
crowds and the laughter and take her place among them.

Now she saw that to have gone in alone, forcing herself
to perform a purely mechanical act of entering life, would
have proven a sad and hollow gesture. It would have taken
enormous courage that would have come to nothing, for
she would still have been—alone. Imprisoned. Isolated.
But Adam—and how could she ever thank him for this?—
had come along to take her hand and help her; Adam was
showing her the art of participation, the technique, so that
her courage need not again be wasted. She was here now
among the beautiful participants of the world, and she was
truly here because with Adam she was a part of humanness, she too was talking and laughing, no longer outside
looking through a glass window with her nose pressed
longingly against the pane.

Was it this innocence of a Cinderella that drew Adam?
They totally balanced each other, she reflected, this man
who had opened himself to life and lived fully and freely to
the point of near-satiation; and herself, the woman who had
been closed to experience for so long that the world now
burst upon her with the freshness of a miracle. Experience
and Innocence . . . at the end of either route lay despair, did
it not? Perhaps this was the very real bond between them,
the suffering implied by either extreme.

"Whither next?" she asked of Adam, smiling.

He glanced at his watch. "It's after three. What do your
gallery feet suggest?"

"There's that gorgeous exhibit of Danish exports—
and," she added helpfully, "it's very nearby."

"Excellent. Then after that we can retire to our hotels,
meet for cocktails at seven, and decide upon our evening."

"Our evening," she said, laughing. "Oh these evenings
that begin when mine used to be nearly ending!"

"Was it really that narrow a life?"

"Unbelievably so," she told him, but not wanting to
spoil the moment by discussing it. She was thinking how

well Adam managed everything—wines, foods, taxis—
and how creative life could be if a person met all the un-
knowns and stripped them of fears. Because the unknown,
she mused, was made up of many small perils to the self,
such as meeting headwaiters and wine stewards as well as
more significant risks. Charles, she thought, would be
thoroughly unnerved at encountering a maître d', and he
could never be persuaded into an elegant European restaurant: he would rather meet a snarling tiger than a wine
steward, for from the tiger he could retreat with an amused
and lofty smile, knowing himself homo sapiens, the supe-
rior, but a wine steward would confront him with his cow-
ardice in the face of the unknown, the mysterious, and the
worldly.

But Charles had so arranged his life that he would never
meet either, thus drawing the circle closer until the total
withdrawal became accomplished. And then one day—
voilà! she thought sadly—the circle became a noose.

They arose and Adam guided her toward the steps. "In-
cidentally, you're not being followed by an irate husband
or a psychotic admirer, are you?" he asked with a smile.

She laughed. "No, why?"

"Chap strolling by on the path up there—see him?
Short chap in woolly brown tweed. Extremely woolly
tweed."

Melissa saw him and nodded.

"By the sheerest of coincidences he was standing in the
lobby of the State Museum when we left, a mile or two
across town."

"Small world." She was amused. "He's certainly the
least distinguished man I've seen in months. How on earth
could you have noticed him?"

Adam said with distaste, "I have never seen a more
atrociously cut suit—look at it!—and he has the shockingly bad taste to wear a silk tie with it."

She burst out laughing. "What a fastidious person you
are!"

"It is one of my least attractive traits, yes." He was
quite serious, and glancing at him she became aware again

of the ruthlessness underlying his charm; noted it and accepted it without either rationalizing it away, excusing it or censuring it. He was, quite simply, Adam.

The man was standing uncertainly beside the path. As they mounted the steps, they came nearly face to face with him until he turned aside to light the cigarette he was fingering. He had a thin pale face and wore rimless spectacles, he looked like a clerk who worked in a sunless, underground archive. Unobtrusive was indeed the word for him, thought Melissa, unless—she amended with humor —one had an eye for badly cut tweeds. They strolled past, arm in arm.

"Try escargots," he suggested. "They're snails, you know. Have escargot and you will be a woman of the world."

"Just like that," she marveled.

"Just like that."

"Then order me snails."

"Madame will have *Vinbjergsnegle*," he told the waiter.

"We seem always to be eating," she pointed out.

"On the contrary we have visited the State Museum, the Glyptopek which you had already seen, lunched in Tivoli —a cultural experience in itself—and visited shops in which the displays may very well have outdone the museums."

"I know. The color of their pottery and glass!" She shook her head in awe. "Unbelievable. I think the Danes invent new color wheels, my palette will have to be much brighter after this."

"I wish I might see some of your work."

"Perhaps one day you will—I plan a very good new life." Even as she said this she was aware of the bravado behind her words.

"You are fortunate to have your work."

It was all that she would have now, but she could not confess this even to herself. "You enjoy yours?"

"Very much so." He nodded. "And I enjoy life."

She smiled. "I know that. Is there anything you've not had?"

"I've never loved," he said simply.

She looked at him closely. "The one experience missing in a lifetime of experiences . . ."

"Yes—and the only truly fulfilling one."

She sighed. "I think—so very often—of how the word is flung about by young lovers, by Madison Avenue, by ministers and priests. And only a very few people are capable of love. Of intoxications but not love." She looked at him thoughtfully. "You're honest to admit it. Most people pretend, as I did. They spend their whole lives pretending they love."

"And feel nothing," he agreed.

She said wistfully, "Perhaps if one knows—and wants very much to love—it becomes a possibility. Do you feel all the things that happen to you?" she asked curiously.

"Oh, life touches me," he said. "Yet I can feel neither love nor hate. Somehow the spectrum of my emotions is limited."

"Are you a sentimentalist?"

"Yes."

She nodded. "Yes, I think you are. I think—I decided this all by myself—that sentiment is often a substitute for love."

"How so?"

"It feels more like a hanging-on, and involves a dwelling on the past. Love, I think, is a letting go. Never destructive, never possessive or clinging."

"Is it?" he asked. "You see I don't know."

"I don't know either," she said slowly.

It was nearly midnight when they emerged from the restaurant. "Could you be persuaded to walk?" he asked.

"No persuasion needed, I'd prefer it."

They turned to the left, crossing the Raadhuspladsen to enter the now-quiet Frederiksbergg. "Funny," said Adam, "there's that chap again—I swear it's the same one. We just passed him. The Pale One."

The Pale One. It was strange that she knew at once who

Adam meant, and turning quickly she was just in time to
catch the gleam of rimless spectacles before the man halted
to peer into a shop window. A little breath of fear touched
Melissa, light as the stroke of a feather, and then she
turned to Adam and said with a laugh, "A tourist with the
same list that we have."

"Obviously," he said with amusement. "Small city,
Copenhagen."

At the hotel he did not pause in the lobby. When she
glanced inquiringly at his face, he said, "I'll come and tuck
you into bed." She nodded. This, too, seemed right and
natural.

# 5

It was nearly ten o'clock when Melissa left the dining room the next morning and crossed the lobby to the lounge where Adam would meet her following his own morning ablutions. Sunlight streamed through the long windows of the nearly empty room, and her passage to the couch sent dust motes swirling. Melissa sat down, remembering Adam with a joy only slightly haunted by the knowledge that this was their last full day together. She sat and quietly tested her joy against loss. On the couch facing her a portly gentleman read his newspaper, cigar smoke rising in clouds from behind the headlines. As she glanced at him, he neatly folded up his paper, nodded to her and said in accented English, "You'll want to see this, of course."

She frowned, not understanding, until she saw that he held out to her the Paris edition of the *Herald Tribune*. She laughed. "That's very kind of you. How on earth did you guess I'm American?"

His brows lifted in surprise. "But you are, aren't you?"

he announced simply, and as he left the lounge, Melissa
wondered in amusement what aura or climate Americans
carried about with them to betray them. Was it the cut of
her clothes, she mused, or their newness? Was it the way
she walked, a certain style of manner or perhaps only the
sheerness of her stockings? She turned to the newspaper,
noting idly that it was two days old. Then she realized that
two days ago at this hour she had not met Adam yet, it
occurred to her that two days really could be a long time,
and she opened the paper to see what other world-shaking
events might have occurred on Tuesday, June 30th. Leafing
through its pages she suddenly halted in astonishment as
she found herself staring at a very clear picture of the man
Stearns.

She had not seen him since that night on A deck. The
eyes in the photograph stared straight into hers and she had
the strange sensation that she had stopped breathing. How
peculiar to meet him in a French newspaper and what was
he doing here? The picture had the bright, painfully stiff
look of a passport photograph. Above it a small headline
said AMERICAN DIES AT SEA. Below it was the name
J. J. Stearns.

"Dead?" she thought blankly. He couldn't be dead. She
smoothed out the paper and forced her attention to the
words under the caption. She read:

CHERBOURG: July 1. The body of J. J. Stearns, an
American, is being held in Cherbourg pending further
identification and notification of kin. Mr. Stearns, 41,
died suddenly aboard the *Bremen* a few hours before it
docked. His destination was listed as Cherbourg and his
home address as New York, N.Y. An autopsy is being
performed.

She whispered, "It can't be true." She remembered that
Stearns had said, he had said—she had an awful feeling
that she was going to burst into tears. "But he has no *right*
to be dead," she thought stupidly, and felt suddenly lost, as
if his death cut her adrift from something secure. He had

said that he might not reach Majorca and now he was dead. What did that mean? He had said . . . but now when she groped for the words Stearns had used she felt vaguely threatened by something formless and oppressive. She thought instead, angrily, "But he had no right to just—just *die*." He had left his package with her, the book about which she knew nothing, and now she was forced to recall that it was in her possession and that she had promised to deliver it for him.

What really had she intended to do with it? She didn't know. She had not been thinking clearly at all when she accepted the package from him. She'd certainly not taken the man seriously; she had been carried away by the moment, by his sense of urgency, but above all by her dislike of disappointing people. So long as the man existed somewhere in this world his errand had remained of little consequence, it had seemed even superfluous, but now he was dead. Had she really cherished the thought that so long as he was alive she might return it to him? What was she to do with his book?

But most staggering of all was the realization that he had said he might not reach Majorca—and then he had died. What did it mean?

She again picked up the paper to stare incredulously at the small photograph. "I am terribly sorry for him," she thought mechanically. "He really was young to die. Of course I'm sorry for him, that's why I'm so upset."

This was better: she began to think of how young he was to die, and how unfortunate it was that he was dead. As she sat there, a conversation overheard days ago slipped suddenly into her mind as if it had been waiting for this moment:

*They hushed it up, of course, shipping companies just don't approve of passengers dying aboard ship.*

*Old man, I suppose . . .*

*No, quite young, the steward said. No more than forty. Suddenly fell to the floor in the corridor—made a terrible sound—and died at once. . . .*

"But that's a heart attack," Melissa thought, and she felt

an enormous, overwhelming sense of relief—except why
did she feel such relief when she was so sincerely sorry
about his death? She thought quickly, "He had a heart con-
dition, that's it, of course. Angina pectoris, perhaps, and
the attacks were growing more frequent and he had a sense
of foreboding . . . Perhaps he was psychic about his death;
some people are. . . ."

She saw a man crossing the lobby and she thought, "I
know that man." It was Adam, and she realized with a
sense of shock how far away she had been to forget that
she was waiting for him, and that this was their last day
together.

As they walked up the avenue arm in arm she said,
"Adam, tell me something."

He smiled. "Tell me what it is that I am to tell you."

"No, be serious," she told him with a smile. "I want you
to pretend something. You're traveling—as you are at this
moment—but perhaps aboard a ship, let's say, and on your
last day out—"

"On my last day out—"

"Yes, a gentleman with whom you've exchanged a few
remarks asks to speak to you alone. Now you are going,
say, to Hong Kong," she said firmly. "Not right away to
Hong Kong, but in a few days. And this gentleman says
that his destination is also Hong Kong but he feels that he
may not get there, he implies that he's a secret agent and
asks you to deliver a small package for him."

Adam smiled and shook his head. "When on earth do
you find the time to read such novels! But go on . . ."

"That's about it for part one," she said, her heart ham-
mering. "He gives you the address and he gives you a
small package, which is a book, and he asks you to deliver
this at a Hong Kong address—"

"Which of course I would not do," said Adam firmly,
and when she stopped and looked at him he added lightly,
"You did say this was happening to *me*. I would agree to no
such thing!"

"Oh," she said, flushing. "But why do you say that?"

She had been about to leap ahead to the man's death and his interruption took her aback.

He said patiently, "You are an absolute innocent, my dear. You've just told me that I don't know the man well."

"Yes, but if he implied he was a secret agent and that it was terribly important—"

Adam laughed. "Why should I believe him? He is still almost a total stranger, is he not? It would be different if I knew his character and background, but if such a stranger had the affrontery to approach me I would compliment him upon concocting a very romantic story, tell him in no uncertain terms that he underestimated my intelligence, and suggest that the man find someone more trusting and more gullible than I."

Melissa's flush deepened. "But—why gullible, Adam?"

"I see that I am rapidly disillusioning you. I don't mean to sound callous but it's only common sense not to trust without verification. We Europeans have learned in a hard school, from wars down to simple smuggling. It is you Americans who remain determinedly naïve and impressionable—after all, you have had only Indians to cope with!

"But this whole supposition is unrealistic," he continued. "This chap of yours would never dare to seek me out, he'd look for an American." He smiled at her. "And if he could find one like *you*, my dear—inexperienced, unworldly, as well as traveling alone—"

His words stung her and Melissa's heart sank: the implication was obvious. Had it really been like that, she wondered? For just a moment she wanted to protest, feeling that somehow it was not as Adam pictured it, but now she found herself trapped. To argue the point, to promote a long discussion, would be tiresome to the extreme if it was to remain a hypothetical situation. But if she removed the hypothesis then she would have to admit to Adam that she had indeed been shockingly trusting and gullible. He might be appalled, he might say with a shudder, "But you are an absolute child," and this was true but he had found her a delight. On this last day with him she could not show herself to him as a fool. It was painful enough to see the

situation through Adam's eyes—and Adam was experienced, while she remained the perfect accomplice that he
had described: unworldly, inexperienced, and traveling
alone. Her cheeks were still flaming with embarrassment.

She said lightly, to end it, "Thank you, I was interested
in your reaction."

"But why?" he asked, genuinely puzzled now.

"It doesn't matter," she said quickly, and then, "Oh,
look at that terribly dignified man with cane and attaché
case riding his bicycle! Did you see him, Adam?"

She could not bore him, nor could she impose upon him
as Stearns had already imposed upon her. It was the whole
point of her trip to learn how to manage life alone. Away,
Stearns, she thought, and turned her thoughts resolutely
toward Adam, knowing that nothing—*nothing*—must
corrupt the beauty of their last day together.

# 6

Again they came to Tivoli, to the outdoor café, and Adam ordered beer and they feasted on long open sandwiches, feeding the crumbs to the swans. "Our swans," Adam said, smiling at her.

She laughed. "Do you think they'd agree with you? But if you insist on being sentimental—!"

"I warned you that I'm a sentimental man." He hesitated and then he said suddenly, "What do you think will happen to you, what kind of life will you have? Will you, for instance, have to live frugally?" His voice sharpened with exasperation. "Damn it, what will it be like for you?"

She was touched and made shy by his concern. "I honestly don't know," she said.

"I want you to do something for me. I want to hear from you, say, at Christmastime. I want to know how things go with you, and if you're all right."

His words startled her. She had not expected this from him, in fact she had rigidly schooled herself against expectations of any kind, and now she looked at him with skepticism. "Do you think that's best?"

"I shall want to hear," he said, and reaching across the table he grasped her hand. Shutting out the swans, the people around them, and the gardens, he said harshly, "Don't you realize that you can never be just someone I met in Copenhagen? Do you think I will ever forget you, Melissa?"

She turned deeply scarlet, suddenly lost, for realness so evaded her that she had no means of judging such words and she was both appalled by them—did he really want her to take them seriously?—and frightened by the effect they had upon her. She had flatly made up her mind to expect nothing from him, and now he was offering her something, which bewildered her; for if he genuinely cared, why did he not offer her *more*, and if he did not care, why did he offer her *anything*? She stared at him with absolute helplessness, conflict rendering her mute while wave after wave of scarlet flooded her cheeks.

He said softly, smiling at her, "I have just touched one of those barbed wire fences, I think."

She smiled faintly, and the tension passed. Flippantly, driving him away from her, she said, "I'd not planned on immortality, you see."

He ruefully shook his head. "I should have chosen that other girl on the tour bus." He released her hand and leaned back, his eyes tender. "I should have. She would have proven supremely forgettable, while in you there is an honesty—" He smiled, and picking up the salt shaker he leaned over and sprinkled it on her head. "There," he said. "Now you are not so sweet."

It broke the spell. "Idiot," she laughed, and they stabbed out their cigarettes, gathered up packages and left the café hand in hand.

Later, wandering, she thought dreamily, "This is the day when we shape what is ours." It was as if they both knew how little time remained and must telescope into hours what other lovers browsed through timelessly. To speak of marriages or disillusionments was oddly distasteful today; that belonged to yesterday when they had laid the solidity on which today's lightheartedness was built. Hand in hand they wandered through the Tivoli arcades, making faces into bulging mirrors that showed them elongated, truncated, headless, or torsoless. They bought Tivoli coins and inserted them into gambling machines and watched peaches, pears, apples, bananas spin past. They left Tivoli and walked through the Saxograde, peering into old clothes shops, copper shops, butcher shops. They laughed and were young, and when they touched upon serious things it was books they had read, or plays seen. Nothing existed for them now but today.

"How did you happen to be born in Greece?" she asked. They were dining at a penthouse restaurant overlooking the canals and they sat side by side so that they might watch the boats. In the dusk the lights of the boats were like underwater jewels moving sluggishly, laboriously past them.

Adam shrugged. "My father was also an archaeologist, and very rarely in England. Turkey, Mesopotamia, Greece, Egypt—"

Burrill... her mind seized, lost and then grasped the name. "Not—Sir John Burrill?"

"You've read of him then. Yes, that was my father."

"But what a fantastic childhood you must have had!"

He said dryly, "I never knew him. He was sixty when I was born—my mother was a very young third wife—and he died when I was two years old. Perhaps you recall the story about his death?"

"Something—a curse, wasn't it—because he opened a tomb?"

His lips curved ironically. "It makes a pretty story, although I imagine it was a heart attack, curses or not."

"Are you a sir, too?" she asked.

"No." He said it flatly, almost viciously and she did not—dared not—intrude. Then he smiled. "I'm sorry, I feel extremely ambivalent toward my father. I've never forgiven him for dying."

"So I see! Yet even as you reject him you follow in his footsteps . . ."

"Of course."

She said mischievously, "Dr. Szym would have a very good time with you, I think. But it must also have been difficult for your mother," she added soberly.

"She survived. After a number of lovers she took a second husband, a racing car enthusiast much younger than herself."

"Then perhaps she didn't survive," Melissa pointed out tartly.

He shrugged. "Perhaps. I don't know. I only know that it was a rather untidy mess to grow up with. Unfortunately her second husband drove very fast even when he was not racing and they were both killed in a car crash when I was seventeen."

"Now that's a rotten beginning for you," she admitted and looked at him, measuring him in the light of this new knowledge.

It was so difficult to imagine his past; nationality and differences of definition intruded, for they each met out of context and in groping toward an understanding of the other's history were reduced to labeling and classifying. Adam, for instance, had never visited America. He could say of her, "She is an artist but before that she was the daughter of a small-town New England dentist, and then she married another small-town New England dentist" and with what could he equate this culturally in his own country? He knew that she could afford a psychiatrist and a trip to Europe but he must realize that her clothes were not expensive. When he asked if she would have to live frugally did he think she would have to give up ski trips to Sun Valley every winter, or give up one of her three meals a day? If he knew that she had sold thirty shares of American Telephone and Telegraph stock to bring her here, would he suppose that she cut coupons in a bank vault every week, or would he understand that in America professional men often bequeathed thirty shares of A.T. & T. to their daughters and that actually this meant very little at all. She, in turn, knowing of his prized collection of antiquities, his knighted father, his Mercedes-Benz and his affairs with women, immediately, by American standards, labeled him as rich—even playboy rich—when in the Mediterranean countries this might not be so at all. How was one to know? She realized for the first time how people depended upon symbols and groups for identification; she and Adam had each left their groups and symbols behind them, and perhaps this too contributed to the intensity of their meeting because symbols were depersonalizing and groups confining.

"I'm sorry," she said with feeling, and suddenly she wanted to reach out and touch his hand lying very near hers on the table. It was a square, brown hand with compact creative fingers and she stared at it, willing herself to touch it. She even forced the muscles of her hand to tighten, and feeling the muscles obey, she urged them toward Adam's hand. Yet they could not move, they dared not. Her lips tightened. This hand at which she stared had held hers, this hand of Adam's had made love to her, yet still she could not spontaneously reach out to express what she felt in a simple gesture of friendship. She remained locked up, contained, acted upon, but unacting.

She lay in his arms, replete with laughter and tenderness and sated desire so that she was liquid, almost without flesh, like someone who had melted into the night. Yet she was at the same time deeply aware of her body and of his as they lay side by side, touching only a little for companionship and out of memory of what they had created together. "My body is wiser than I," she thought, but still at this moment she was glad that he left in a few hours because another day, another night, and she might lose the sense of separateness that she so desperately tried to maintain, like a child learning a new language. And losing it, she might also lose control and become a beggar, asking too much.

Adam stirred and sat up. "I feel very sad," he said

abruptly. He turned and looked down at her with sadness etched into the lines of his face. He said huskily, "You have to be someone very special to affect me like this."

"Are you sorry?" she asked curiously.

He smiled faintly. "Will you have breakfast with me at eight?"

She nodded.

"I'll leave and let you sleep a few hours in that lamentably narrow bed of yours." Still he hesitated and then he said almost unwillingly, as if the words were wrenched from his being, "With you I know I have come nearer to loving than with any woman in my life."

At his words she felt all of her defenses rise in her, felt herself stiffen to ward off this blow, this assault of tenderness, and then to her astonishment something turned over in her like a child wanting to be born and with tears in her eyes she reached out without restraint and took his hand and held it. His glance dropped and she saw that he remembered and understood, and they remained like this, transfixed by gratitude and tenderness, a quality almost of reverence between them, as if they exchanged benedictions.

Time lay between them now like a wedge. They sat in the lounge of the air terminal and the hours behind them were like a weight that could neither be picked up nor put down. Behind the huge glass window lay a Copenhagen that had been theirs; people still walked its streets, passing that window, yet already for them the town lay behind glass—it no longer belonged to them—for something was ending. She felt it in her throat.

"I loathe good-bys," Adam said huskily.

"Yes." Her voice broke a little.

"I did some arithmetic this morning when I shaved. We met at four o'clock on Tuesday and now it is ten o'clock on Friday morning. We have known each other for sixty-six hours."

"Only that long," she said. "It feels—"

He reached out and grasped her hand. "I know. Don't say it."

But there were now so many things they couldn't say; it was better to resurrect old lovers' jokes and lighten the moment. "We never did see the Tuborg beer factory," she reminded him.

"Or rent a boat."

"Or dance."

"Or swim."

"Or see the Palace, and the Changing of the Guard."

He said impulsively, "Wait here a moment," and got up and walked away and out of sight. When he returned a moment later he was carrying a single long-stemmed red rose. "For you," he said. "Just one to keep you company until you leave Copenhagen, too, tomorrow."

"You think I will remember you only that long?" she asked tremulously.

The loudspeaker burst into excited sound and Adam said in a stifled voice, "They're announcing my bus to the airport."

She nodded and stood up like someone facing sentence of death. She had never seen a man cry, but Adam's eyes were wet with tears. He said unsteadily, "Good-by my love—I'll never forget you. Not ever."

She thought suddenly, "But this is for a lifetime, how can I bear it?" "Oh Adam," she whispered, and flinging her arms about his neck she pressed her cheek to his, feeling the wetness of his tears. Drawing back she looked deeply into his face. "Adam," she said. "Adam, have a *wonderful* life," and she knew in this moment that what she felt was very near to the generosity that is real love.

"God bless you, my darling," he whispered.

A little sob escaped her and she turned and plunged away from him, hurrying desperately now to end it. But with a hand on the door to the street she remembered that this was forever, and she dared to turn and look again. Briefly, wordlessly, they gazed at each other for that last time across the air terminal.

"Good-by," she thought, tears streaming down her

cheeks. Tenderly, sadly, she lifted the rose he had given her in a final salute and then she walked out, sheltering the rose before her like a candle.

The hotel room was empty and silent. She had forgotten how empty a hotel room could be. She took only a few steps inside it and stopped: the emptiness was an affront, it was a slap across her cheek, it was a vacuum into which she must enter at the cost of losing herself. In the mirror as she closed the door she saw reflected a strange woman with flushed cheeks and wet eyes and she thought, "But I felt so beautiful," and then, peering closer, "What could he have seen in me?" But the reflection held no meaning for her because the room was untenanted, she was not really here.

"Adam," she whispered tentatively, and then, despairingly, "Adam, where have you gone?" But he had vanished into silence, into another void, and was bleakly, utterly lost to her. Forever—it was a word that echoed through whole caverns of endless time, and if an exalted feeling lingered, to what use could it be put, could she really fashion from it a painting or a new life? In this moment there was nothing but herself—herself alone again, and tomorrow she must fly away into still another unknown and go stubbornly on and on, every step taking her farther from Adam.

Was it to fade so soon? She sat down and tried to recall him, repeating like incantations the words he had said, remembering that she had reached out to touch him only a few hours ago, and in this very room. But he was no longer here, no longer possessable, and what was the use of it all if she was alone again?

He had said, "You must be someone very special to affect me like this." And then, "With you I have come nearer to loving than with any other woman in my life."

She thought, "I'm doing exactly what I shouldn't do, I'm mourning him, I'm trying to cling, except now I'm clinging to a memory, and this is all wrong because we were real together." She said aloud, fiercely, "Adam, I will *not* put your memory into a coffin and surround you with flowers and lighted candles, damn it. I will only be proud."

She realized that someone was knocking on her door and she thought with a wild, irrational hope, "Adam has come back?" She opened the door but it was not Adam. A man in uniform stood patiently in the hall. Seeing her he removed his cap. "Madame Melissa Aubrey?"

She nodded blankly. "Yes."

He held out a card to her. "Bojesen of the Copenhagen Police. May I speak to you a moment?"

"Yes, of course," she said uncertainly, and was suddenly aware of the tears in her eyes and the sodden handkerchief in her hand. As he walked inside she said, "You must excuse me, I have just said good-by to a very dear friend. Did you come to check my passport?"

"Partings can be sad, yes," he agreed politely. "No, I do not need your passport, there are a few questions I must ask you." He gestured to the desk and chair. "May I?"

"Of course, but if it's not about my passport—"

He sat down and drew out a small notebook and a pencil. He moistened the stub of the pencil with his tongue, tested it, and peered at words inside the notebook. Melissa leaned against the bureau and then said impatiently, "Yes?" She wanted him gone so that she could go on remembering Adam, and what was this man doing here, anyway?

Reading from his notebook he said, "You are the Melissa Aubrey who entered Denmark on Monday, arriving on the Alpen Express from Hamburg, is this correct?"

"Yes, yes, quite correct."

He nodded. "Yes, that is where your passport was stamped. It has taken us several days to trace you, you see."

"Oh?" she said in surprise.

"It is also correct that you are the Madame Aubrey who arrived in Europe aboard the *Bremen*, which docked Sunday at Bremerhaven?"

Her heart had begun to beat very quickly. "Yes."

"Then you are listed as having"—he peered short-sightedly at his notes—"as having sat at table 43 aboard ship?"

"Yes," she whispered.

"You knew then a man named Stearns...Mr. J. J. Stearns."

A man named Stearns... The name was incongruous in this hotel room so far removed from the ship and yet now that the man had spoken Stearns' name she knew that she had been expecting it. "Yes," she said breathlessly. "Why?"

"Did you know him well?" asked the policeman with a smile.

She had grown rigid and very still; a part of her had moved off at a distance to watch and record the scene and make comments, but she was not certain which Melissa was real. "No," she heard herself say. "None of us knew him well."

"None of us?"

"The others at table 43. There were four college students traveling together from the same midwestern university," she explained. "Do you want their names?"

"Please," he said. "As verification."

She gave him their names and he wrote them down.

"But surely Mr. Stearns conversed with you at meals?"

She shook her head. "No, not at all. That is, except for the usual Good Mornings and Good Evenings, and once in a while a comment or a smile." Staring at the policeman she said suddenly, "I know he is dead, I saw his picture in the newspaper."

"Yes," the man said patiently, almost soothingly. "Now to whom did the man speak?"

"Why are you asking?" pleaded Melissa.

"The French police have asked us to make inquiries," he told her. "We are cooperating with them. Doubtless they are asking these same questions of the others who sat at table 43. Now if you would be so kind—"

"But I never saw him speak to anyone," she told him. "He was not like the others. He never mingled, he was always alone. Sometimes I would see him reading a book in the lounge, or smoking his pipe on deck, but always alone."

"He never spoke to you personally, that is to you individually, alone?"

"No," she said quickly, making it true, forcing it to be true. "But why?"

He held up his hand, saying, "Only two more questions, please. Just when did you last see Mr. Stearns aboard ship, if you remember?"

She said with a trace of irritation, "Since I saw him only at meal times then I suppose it would have been at the last meal he shared with us."

He wrote this down slowly and carefully. "Now if you please, your addresses while you are in Europe." He added with an apologetic smile, "It really has been difficult, this finding you. There are so many hotels in Copenhagen!" She nodded and gave him dates and the names of hotels.

"Thank you. You understand this is routine," he told her, putting away his notebook and pencil. "I am sorry to have disturbed you."

"But you've not told me why," she said impatiently. "He died of a heart attack, didn't he?" The man stood up. "Didn't he?" she repeated.

He said primly, "The police do not customarily investigate the deaths of men who die of heart attacks."

"You mean—not a heart attack," she whispered.

With a hand on the door he removed his notebook and flipped it open. Peering at words inside he said, "The autopsy uncovered traces of a poison that simulates a heart attack—but of course that means he had been murdered." Putting on his hat he went out, closing the door behind him.

"Murdered," she echoed, staring at the closed door, and the word had a sour taste to her tongue and an unreal sound in this quiet hotel room. It was a word—no matter how grotesque—that she could no longer escape, and she felt shattered by its finality.

She walked to the closet and brought out her suitcase and resolutely removed from it the book that had belonged to Stearns. She stared at it for several minutes, holding it, weighing it in one hand and pondering its title: *Basic Se-*

*lections from Emerson: Essays, Poems and Apothegms.* It
still seemed a joke to her. He should never have given it to
her—never, she thought fiercely—but still it was here, a
gift from a dead man. A madman as well as a dead one,
she thought, because really it was difficult to fit Stearns
into any conceivable frame of reality. Her encounter with
him had been too bizarre, too sudden and brief to be real.
He had spoken to her for only a few minutes and then he
had left and she had never seen him again. Had he really
happened to her? He must have existed because now he
was dead—they said he was dead—but for her the only
proof lay in this book he had given her. Now she opened it,
trying to remember Stearns and to make him real. Turning
the pages slowly she tapped and poked at the binding but
still there was nothing concealed in it, there were no
dummy pages or hollow spaces. It remained, quite absurdly, a book.

If it was only a book, she thought bleakly, then Adam
was wrong.

Stearns, on the other hand, had said it was a book—a
book with something of value on page 191.

She turned to page 191. The page contained—she
counted them—ten apothegms, each with numbers at the
end of the quotations. The first apothegm read, "One who
wishes to refresh himself by contact with the bone and
sinew of society must avoid what is called the respectable
portion of his city or neighborhood with as much care as in
Europe a good traveler avoids American and English people. ('45–42–VII–66)"

There were nine other quotations, each with numbers at
their conclusion. She turned to the first page of the apothegms and learned that the numbers following each quota-
tion indicated the year in the 1800's in which the item was
entered in Emerson's journal, his age at the time, the
number of the volume in which it appeared, and the page
number.

She thought, "I should have told Adam about this from
the very beginning. I went about it all wrong because I was
afraid. Afraid to make it real even to myself." It had been

the security of Adam's presence that had distracted her
from the seriousness of it, but now Adam was gone and
she was frightened.

She looked at the book again, and her own earlier conclusions returned but now they swept back to take root with
force and conviction. She thought, "If this really is a
code?" and then, "If Stearns really *was* an agent—"

The room felt suddenly suffocating to her. She picked
up her coat and went out again, walking very quickly but
whether to escape her thoughts or to find Adam she didn't
know. It was raining but she scarcely noticed as she turned
blindly up one street and then another. She found herself in
front of Adam's hotel and stopped—if she went inside
would his ghost still be there, would there be traces of him
left that she could talk to?—and then she reached the inter-
section where they had met that first morning and she stood
on the corner with her hand at her throat, remembering.
She realized that she ought not to have left her hotel. "This
city is dead now—he's gone," she thought. "Everything
has ended. There has even been a policeman questioning
me since Adam left. I'm being hurled back into a world I
don't understand." She shivered. "I wish I could talk to
Adam, he would know what to do." She turned to hurry
back to the hotel and, in turning, bumped into a man behind her. She stared at him incredulously—at the pale be-
spectacled face, the woolly, brown tweed suit, the silk
tie—and was almost bewildered by the impact of seeing
him again. This man had been a lovers' joke between her
and Adam yet on another level, from the very first, she had
been aware of this fear in her, this flaw of doubt, this
consternation when they met. Now Adam was gone,
Stearns was not only dead but poisoned, and the man was
still here.

The Pale One bowed quickly, an instinctive gesture of
apology, and hurried past with his head down. She stood
and watched until he vanished from sight. She remembered
that it was Adam who had pointed the man out to her.
Adam had noticed him first—at the State Museum, wasn't
it?—and then The Pale One had been at Tivoli and she too

had seen him—standing, as if he waited for them—and again that night he had been a shadow behind them when they left *The Seven Nations* and walked up the Frederiksbergg.

But, perversely, he had not been seen at all yesterday, and so he had remained a coincidence, someone glimpsed a number of times in the space of one day and then not again. She thought desperately, "If only we had seen him once more while we were together—" But even now she was not sure that she would have dared name her fears to Adam.

She reached her hotel and then her room and locked the door behind her. And now—*now,* too late!—the words she had buried came back to her with blinding clarity. "Why me?" She had asked Stearns, and he had replied, "Because I begin to suspect that I may not get through to Majorca."

And then, urgently, "There may be others after this; if they put two and two together, if they know for instance that you also go to Majorca, and that we sat at the same table . . ."

"*Others* . . . oh God," she thought, and caught in her breath sharply, feeling her body writhe as if even physically she had to retreat from the implication of those words. But when she had been with Adam those very same words, remotely recalled, had appeared laughable: how was this possible? Now they assumed frightening authority in this lonely hotel room because she was alone again, as she had been alone when she met Stearns. And now Stearns was dead—*murdered*—and she had just seen The Pale One again. It was like a nightmare. Life was moving too quickly for her; she felt like a figure strapped to a chair in front of a moving picture screen and forced to endure the accelerated images of nightmare events that one after another rushed at her from the screen. She must get out of Copenhagen.

She went to the window and looked out but there was no one standing below watching, as they did in the movies. She sat down on the bed and put her head into her hands, wishing she was not such a hollow of innocence, wishing she had solidity inside and wasn't so unlived, so unsure. There must be people who could say of her encounter with Stearns "Yes, you *should* be frightened," or "No, you are imagining too much," but she couldn't evaluate it, it was all too difficult to grasp when so many of her small terrors were projections of her fear of aloneness.

Suddenly nothing felt real, not even the bed upon which she sat, and she lifted her head because if nothing was feeling real then it meant that she was losing touch again. "Dr. Szym, where are you," she whispered despairingly, or did she mean God, or were they intermingled now, these two symbolic Caring Ones, except neither of them was real because they were not here, and if they weren't here then they didn't care, either.

It was going to be a very bad attack, she realized, gritting her teeth: everything slippery, sliding around, coated with glass, untouchable, unfeelable, unpossessable, unreal.

If there were just one person—one person—to whom she could turn—

There wasn't. There never would be. She began to pace the floor and then she sat down and gripped the arms of the chair, forcing herself to unclench the muscles of her knotted stomach, and to expand her lungs with deep slow breaths. Slowly, softly, she literally drew together the pieces of her torn self until presently the intolerable became almost endurable. After this she cried and knew the luxury of feeling again, and then came anger—the blessed healing catharsis of anger—and she became a person again.

# 7

THE PLANE WAITED ON THE FIELD LIKE A SMALL SILVER
bird. Staring at it Melissa thought with dismay, "*This* is
what will lift me from Copenhagen to Paris?" and she regarded it with fascinated revulsion, knowing that she had
to deliver herself to it with no trust at all. She felt already
diminished by the loss of her suitcase. They had taken it
from her inside the terminal, given it a small numbered tag
and dropped it at the lip of a dark chute that had instantly
carried it away, surely never to be seen again. How could
she possibly trust a numbered paper tag to carry her be-
longings from Copenhagen to Paris when the world was so
huge, and how could she trust this plane to carry her safely
to Paris when it was so small? She had never before realized the extent of trust needed for traveling. As she
mounted the steps to the plane, she resigned herself to both
the loss of her suitcase and her life, and of the two she felt
the more peevishly involved with the suitcase, which had
been *taken* from her, for in such moments of anxiety the
symbol became more real than the actual.

"I will be strong for Adam," she thought, forgetting that it was for herself that she had to be strong, and then to comfort herself: "If this plane takes me away from Adam at least it also removes me from The Pale One."

She sat down in her seat over the wing, and presently stood up to allow a slender blond boy to take the seat beside her. When each of them began at the same time to read the instructions for emergency landings, and then to examine seat belts, Melissa said with a faint smile, "Your first trip by air?"

He looked at her and grinned. "Yes. It is perhaps yours, too?" He spoke in careful schoolboy English.

She nodded. "Yes. We will suffer together then."

He was from a small town in Denmark, he said, and he was going out of his country for the first time, to Paris to join a film company in which his cousin had a position. "He has got for me a small acting part."

She nodded, seeing what appeal he would have. He was very attractive, very innocent and guileless and young. "Perhaps you will become a star," she suggested.

His smile shared with her the absurdity of such a pretentious thought yet implied dreams already dreamed of such a hope. "It would be—like a fairy tale, no?" he said softly.

"Very definitely."

"And you—you are an American?" he asked.

"Yes."

"Perhaps I get to America, too," he said, smiling shyly, warmly.

She felt better for the young man's presence, it made all the difference to her between panic and calm. Why was it, she wondered, that with people she could be so friendly; shy of course and yet, once welcomed, so infinitely compassionate and whole; did she draw nourishment from them?

"Yes—like a parasite," she reminded herself bitterly, for it was reassurance they gave her, the reassurance that she existed. With apologies to Descartes they *saw* her, therefore she *was*, but when they left they took her with them, leaving only a shell behind. Yet she remembered that on a few occasions she had experienced wholeness when she was alone: it had happened very briefly at times during therapy, when something inside of her had knitted together, all tension had fled, and she had experienced a deep tranquillity; and one night on the ship, in the midst of terror at disembarking, there had come the sensation of a hand placed gently upon her heart, soothing her, and she had lain in her berth and reflected quietly upon all the people she had ever known and they had felt very real and close to her, a part of her for always. But then they had gone away, leaving her empty and alone again. Had they been real, did they still exist somewhere? It was so difficult to know if one was uncertain of one's own existence. . . .

A voice came over the loudspeaker and Melissa felt the boy stiffen beside her. They listened together as the pilot introduced himself, described their route and cheerfully asked them to fasten their seat belts. The plane began to move. It taxied down the long runway and came to a stop. Melissa waited, a dreadful excitement gripping her. She started to say, "I think perhaps now—" and then the plane seemed to pull itself together, it moved with purpose, like a rubber band released from a sling. Feeling both frightened and exhilarated Melissa looked beyond the window, saw the runway blur, heard a strident, deafening, whistling noise, and then the ground began to fall away from them. As they climbed higher she turned to look at the boy and they exchanged embarrassed, optimistic, congratulatory smiles. "I think we're up," she said.

"Yes, I think so."

They were indeed up, the plane banking for its sweep over Copenhagen, and as Melissa leaned with the plane against the blue sky she felt something break with joy inside of her, as if all her fears had been contained in a small compartment which pure sensation had shattered. "But it is a beautiful thing to fly," she thought in astonishment and at this moment of release, this sensation of purest freedom, she looked down upon her life and could not understand why she had made of it such a stunted, haunted affair. She saw life to be as limitless as the sky, a tapestry into which brilliantly colored possibilities could be woven into patterns of grandeur. She felt dimensions of her mind dissolve, open up, slip aside so that she was able to look back upon Adam with joy and gratitude and for the first time to move her thoughts toward the future and meet with no dreads. She was capable of feeling the future, the excitement of its possibilities, and the splendor of its choices. It was for this then that she had been freed: this joy of life, this exaltation; it was this that had been confined during all those years of burial until decay hurled her back to life. Words came to her from Millay's *Renascence*: "the world stands out on either side no wider than the heart is wide, Above the world is stretched the sky, no higher than the soul is high." Her soul felt very high, her heart very wide, she felt near to bursting in this moment and scarcely able to contain the beauty of the world.

Tenderly she brought out her sketchbook and pen, and for the sheer joy of it interrupted the stillness of a white page with slashing lines of ink. Another, and then another: colors spun through her head dizzily—if only she had canvas and paint! At last, joy settling into contentment, she began to place the profile of the boy on paper: the mop of bright golden hair, the tenderness of his profile, the dreams in his eyes.

"But you are an artist," he said, turning to watch.

"Yes," she agreed blissfully.

"We are both artists then."

"Yes." She said it flatly, without equivocation.

He said solemnly, "I intend to be a very good actor."

She paused and looked at him, nodding. "And I am going to be a very good painter."

He smiled and they both broke into delighted laughter, two children sharing in blood-oaths, and tearing the inked-in portrait from her notebook she thrust it at him. "From a very great painter to a very great actor," she told him. "In memory of our first plane ride."

* * *

Melissa and the boy parted at Le Bourget, formally shaking hands at the passport counter and wishing each other well. Later, following him toward the gates, she saw him warmly embraced by two men as bright-headed and Scandinavian as he, and she slowed her pace to watch, admiring the family scene. But when her gaze moved past and beyond them she caught in her breath sharply and froze. She thought for an instant that she had seen The Pale One hurrying through the doors but that was impossible, her imagination was playing tricks on her for The Pale One had been firmly left behind in Copenhagen. How could he be here—indeed how *could* he?—when he had certainly not been on the plane with her and could not know her destination even if he had been aware of her departure. Was she going to imagine him everywhere, she wondered?

She resumed walking, humorously resigned to the fact that every small man with glasses and a pale face would for a time remind her of her Copenhagen phantom. Feeling lighthearted again, she walked out of the building and climbed into the bus that would take her to the heart of the city.

She had reached Paris, and in her very survival there was surprise and joy.

At Air Invalides she converted Danish money into French, and went by taxi to her hotel, a small, family-run affair on the Left Bank, chosen by her long ago for some reason already forgotten—doubtless as another exercise in self-sufficiency, she thought now, wryly. Entering its doors she was disheartened by its smallness, however; she saw at once that it lacked a dining room to which she could repair when she tired of ordering omelet, the sitting room was prim and small, there was almost no lobby and the elevator was no larger than a closet.

"Ah—oui, Madame Aubrey," murmured the young man behind the desk, and going to a door he whistled for the old man who toiled up the stairs from the cellar to grasp Melissa's suitcase and key. She was placed in the narrow wire lift while the man climbed the two flights to her floor —she could see the top of his head as she was carried up with infinite slowness. They met again in a long, dark corridor. "Ze lavatory," he said in difficult English, pointing up the hall. "If you want ze bath you question at ze desk." He unlocked the door and swung it wide for her, placing her suitcase just inside before he went away, closing the door behind him.

Another city, another hotel room... This room was so small it had been impossible to give it style and none had been attempted. Along the left wall stood a large old-fashioned mahogany wardrobe, a small writing table, and a sink. The opposite wall was filled by her couch. Melissa took a few steps into the room and stopped. She knew this feeling, this sudden, curious sense of lostness, this sadness. "We are becoming friends, this feeling and I," she thought with a smile, but it was different now—all of her life was going to be different now—because she carried Adam with her. There could be no panic here.

"You must be someone very special," he had said.

"With you I know I have come nearer to loving than with any woman in my life," he had said.

Adam was proof to her that the unknown lying just around the corner could be beautiful as well as frightening. Adam was proof to her that she could be free inside, as she had been free on the plane over Copenhagen when her heart stretched beyond all boundaries.

"I will attack Paris with zest," she thought, and decided to go out very quickly, before the sadness of their parting returned and before this strange and empty room came to feel more safe to her than what lay outside. She must do a very good job with Paris... as Adam would do.

Only a block away lay the Seine, and across its splintered brightness she could see the towers of Notre Dame. She began to walk along the quay, map in hand, realizing that Paris contained more light and sky and water than she had ever imagined. Yet its people looked more strange and foreign to her than any that she had seen so far, even in Denmark: they seemed to her a race apart, like Martians. This was the Left Bank, and she saw brutal, sensuous

faces, remote eyes, men with beards, mustaches, turtle-
necks, jeans, string ties, boots, sandals; she saw women
with shorn hair, hair to their waists, slacks, pullovers,
high cheekbones, white lips, pink lips, purple lips. She
reached a boulevard and when she passed a restaurant—
it was already half-past six—she threaded her way
among its outdoor tables and entered the dim interior.
Parisians would dine at eight, she supposed, but she was
hungry. "Diner?" she confidently inquired of the man behind the bar.

"Oui," he said, smiling, and with a nod rang a bell.

From the rear issued a man with a small Chaplinesque
mustache across his upper lip and a white napkin folded
over one arm. He bowed and escorted her into a dining
room empty of all but white-clad tables. Handing her a
menu he spoke rapidly in French.

Melissa looked up at him. She could reply only in pan-
tomine, understanding nothing, and she lifted her arms and
shoulders in an exaggerated and helpless shrug. A twinkle
appeared in the man's eyes. He replied by stepping back
and throwing up his hands in mock horror, his face utterly
deadpan, his eyes amused and twinkling—and going to the
rear he returned with an English menu, depositing it before
her with a bow.

Melissa sipped her vermouth feeling like a queen reign-
ing over an empty kingdom while her waiter—prim again
—stood in the rear with napkin over his arm. But the
moment that she put down her glass he was at her side and
with grave humor they tackled the next course. "Onion
soup," she decided, pointing to the French translation beside the English.

"Mmmm—oui," he cried in congratulatory delight and
presently from the cellar—still with the napkin over his
arm—he brought a tray. It was taken to the rear, plates
wiped and polished with his napkin, and then the steaming
cauldron was brought to her table. With a marvelous flour-
ish that would have leveled any passerby, he deposited
plates before her and filled one with soup, standing by to
await her reaction.

She did not disappoint him. "Oui—mmm," she said, grinning at him.

He bowed solemnly, eyes twinkling back at her.

Steadily, course by course, they moved through the menu until at last Melissa put down her coffee cup and dredged up a long-forgotten word from old French movies. She said to him, "Enchantée!"

He did not smile—she had not yet seen him smile—but his eyes spoke for him, brimming with delight as he bowed. Something had been created, she thought as she left, still smiling; a moment, a mood, a joy. This man had proven to her that Paris was manageable and might even be a delight, and she was grateful. Feeling luxuriously filled with both food and confidence she walked into her hotel and paused at the desk for her key. This evening the attendant was a handsome Frenchwoman whose English was very good. Handing over the key she said, "I am sorry, Madame Aubrey, there was a letter waiting for you this afternoon that my brother did not give you."

Melissa laughed. "No, no, you must be mistaken, no one knows where—"

But the woman did not respond. "It is there, behind you in the letterboxes. There, you see? Your room number is fourteen, do you see box fourteen?" She was leaning across the desk to point with a pencil, determined to see the letter delivered and her responsibility discharged.

There was indeed a white envelope in box fourteen. Melissa thought suddenly, hopefully, *Adam*? Adam had once asked where she was to stay in Paris, but hearing the name of the hotel he had shaken his head, saying it was not a name that he knew. Was it possible that he had memorized the name and written to her? Removing the letter from the box she looked at it. It was indeed for Mrs. Melissa Aubrey but her heart sank for it had arrived airmail from America. Printed in the top left-hand corner were the words *Carmichael Travel Agency, Bruxton, Massachusetts, U.S.A.*

Her travel agents . . . the people who had made out her itinerary for her, and the only people who *would* know

where she was each day of her trip. With a sigh she slit the
envelope and scanned the contents of the brief typewritten
letter.

                                                 June 30th
Dear Mrs. Aubrey,
    Your cablegram startled us this afternoon. Having
only an hour ago cabled your lost itinerary to you, it
occurs to me now that you really should have other
copies in case such an accident happens to you again. I
am therefore enclosing two typed copies, and speeding
them airmail toward your Paris hotel. I suggest that you
carry one in your purse and one in your suitcase. Better
luck this time.
    We all hope you are having a wonderful trip. Do stop
in and tell us about it when you return.
    With all best wishes,

                                          Joe Carmichael


"What on earth," thought Melissa, completely bewildered. She began to read the letter a second time, still
rather stupidly, because she had no idea what Joe Carmichael meant or to what cables he was alluding. "Lost itinerary?" she echoed blankly. "I haven't lost any itineraries."
As if to confirm this she opened her purse and brought out
her typed list of arrivals and departures and displayed it to
an invisible audience. But this was unsatisfying because
the Carmichael Travel Agency was thousands of miles
away and could neither see nor hear her.
    She began reading the letter again. Obviously her travel
agent was laboring under the delusion that she'd lost her
itinerary and that she'd been suspended somewhere in Europe with no idea of where to go next, or on which train or
plane. Laboring under this delusion he had cabled her a
replacement copy. But to whom had he sent it? She'd received no cables from anyone, and certainly not from the
Carmichael Agency.
    She'd certainly not asked for one, either.
    What on earth could they be writing about?

"Now hold on, Melissa," she told herself, and letter in hand went into the small sitting room and sat down. "Try logic," she suggested sternly. Why did they believe her list was lost? Someone had told them so. Charles? But Charles wouldn't use her name, and anyway Charles was in Massachusetts where he obviously was in no position to receive a cablegram addressed to her in Europe.

For that matter, Mr. Carmichael made it clear that the cable signed with her name had come from Europe.

A chill of astonishment gripped Melissa. Someone here in Europe must have cabled Joe Carmichael—in Melissa's name—and then received the cable for her. Someone who wanted to know where she was going, what planes she would be taking, where she was to stay, and for how long.

The Copenhagen police? But they would never have signed her name to a cable even if they had known where to send one. It had taken them three days to trace her from the border to the hotel, the policeman had said so.

Adam? She looked at the date on the letter. But she had already met Adam when this letter was written on July first, and Adam need only have asked.

The Pale One . . .

"Now stop being ridiculous," Melissa thought with scorn. "That was Copenhagen, and you are imagining things again. There is no Pale One in Paris. Besides, how could that little man possibly know about the Carmichael Agency in Bruxton, Massachusetts?"

Letter in hand she left the sitting room and walked into the wire elevator to be carried slowly, majestically to the second floor. She unlocked the door and walked in, tossing coat and key to the bed. No, really, it was inconceivable, she must be losing her grip to think such a thing because there was no possible way of anyone in Europe connecting her with the Carmichael Agency back in America, there was absolutely no—

Her glance fell to her suitcase under the sink and she stiffened. "Oh God," she thought drearily, as her eyes met the first bright label which she had affixed to her suitcase before leaving New York. In clear blue letters printed on

white gum were emblazoned the words CARMICHAEL
TRAVEL AGENCY, BRUXTON, MASSACHUSETTS.
That label had been on her suitcase for two weeks, the
words had moved with her from New York to Bremerhaven, to Hamburg, to Copenhagen, and to Paris, carried
openly through air terminals, railway stations, customs,
and hotel lobbies.

Were they really that clever?

She had almost forgotten Stearns again. Stearns had
happened to her three cities ago in this necklace of countries she was spanning, he and his book were no more than
a suppressed dread now, a blurred shadow on her consciousness.

Was she being followed then in Paris, too? Had it really
been The Pale One at Le Bourget?

She felt suddenly dizzy and sat down, and then as the
full implications of the letter overwhelmed her she felt
abruptly and acutely nauseated. She stumbled to the sink
and was violently ill into the washbasin.

# 8

IT HAD GROWN DARK OUTSIDE. DRAINED AND STUPEFIED, she drew the heavy flowered curtains across the window and sat in the darkness shivering from weakness as well as fear. She had drawn the curtains to take shelter but of course there was no one following her; it was her sick imagination that insisted she was under some kind of surveillance. Life wasn't *like* this. She had arrived here in Paris precisely seven hours ago, and she had been managing splendidly by herself. It didn't make sense to end her evening retching in a hotel basin, it had to be something she'd eaten on the plane or in the restaurant. It couldn't be the letter.

She lighted a cigarette and contemplated the letter that lay open on the writing table across from her. It said—she closed her eyes, repeating the contents to herself, and then to check on her accuracy she reached for the sheet of paper and brought it to the bed with her. *Dear Mrs. Aubrey*—

Yes, she had recalled the words accurately but it was their meaning that eluded her. She could not face the implications. "Look here," she said aloud, as if to God, "I'm just one American tourist traveling abroad for three weeks, why should anything like this happen to *me*?"

"I'm not being followed," she told herself stubbornly. "Why should I be, what have I done?"

And awfullest of all—*who were they*?

She felt exhausted from the conflict going on inside of her. There was a part of her so aware of the letter's meaning that it had sent her, reeling with shock, to the washbasin; and there was a part of her that struggled desperately to find lies with which to conceal and rationalize the situation. For if she accepted the implications of this letter then she would have to acknowledge that The Pale One had been following her in Copenhagen and that he might be following her in Paris, too, that someone knew of her connection with Stearns and that she was therefore in grave danger. But to acknowledge danger was to face terror and loss: the unendurable loss of the small sense of security she must cling to, a loss of her identity and the greatest possible loss of all, her life. In that direction lay panic and disintegration. Nor could she go home. It was not just the money involved in her trip, nor the sense of defeat that would be carried back with her, but she felt utterly helpless about even the mechanics of changing her plans. Where did one go to change reservations? To whom did one speak? It shattered her even to consider such a change.

She crept to the curtains and parted them, half expecting to meet a face on the other side of the pane but there was only darkness and the blank cement wall of the next building. She walked to her door and opened it, but there was no sudden rustle of movement in the empty, dimly lit hall. She went back into her dark room and sat down on the bed, achingly tired and afraid even of the darkness now because there was nothing else on which to focus her fears. After a while in her despair she began to pound her pillow and every blow was a blow at Stearns. She had found someone to blame, and this—mercifully—distracted her.

\* \* \*

She awoke to the sound of a buzzer—it was nearly nine o'clock and the sun was shining. Removing the receiver from the hook she was told in mangled English that she had not breakfasted yet and that breakfast was being served in the small alcove off the lobby. Melissa dressed and went downstairs to discover a room filled with small tables behind the elevator: a woman brought her a decanter of steaming black coffee and a tray of croissants. The coffee had the effect of awakening Melissa from the nightmare of the preceding night so that she began to look upon this new day with curiosity, to admit its existence, and to admit herself as a person into its existence. She began to realize what she must do, and tentatively she drew out her map, feeling crafty and artful and hopeful. It might be possible to exploit desperation, to draw upon the same atavistic cunning that an animal used when it scented danger and must identify it for survival. When she had finished her coffee and cigarette she left the hotel, map in hand, to look for the curved street up which she had wandered in innocence the evening before. Crossing the Boulevard Saint Michel she turned into the Rue Danton and began to walk slowly its narrow thoroughfare, but although she openly consulted her map and stopped frequently to look with interest in the shop windows the real purpose of her trip was not exploration. By carefully choosing the shop windows into which she peered she was trying to observe the people behind her who did not pass her by. It proved more difficult than she'd foreseen because there were already a large number of tourists on the street who shared her inclination to browse among the displays of books, prints and objets d'art. Still, almost all tourists traveled in pairs and before she reached the end of the Rue Danton Melissa had singled out one single, distant shadow that remained stubbornly behind her and was reflected in each window at which she paused. Approaching the end of the street she found what she was looking for—a narrow alley between two shops—and allowing herself to be caught up by a group of camera-slung tourists she walked with them past the alley and then separated herself and ducked in among its shadows.

She stood and waited.

Several people passed, and then the lone man, and there was no longer any doubt: at sight of him Melissa drew in her breath sharply. She knew at last, and was horrified. Certainly if the letter had not alerted her she would never have noticed him—never—for he was no longer wearing woolly brown tweed. The rimless spectacles and the pale thin profile were the same, but in Paris The Pale One had changed to black serge.

Adam would not have approved of this suit, either, she thought with wan humor.

She turned and ran blindly down the alley, barely averting garbage pails, a cat, and a fire escape until she came out upon another street, and then another, and reached the Boulevard Saint Michel and flagged down an empty taxi. "Galerie Lafayette," she gasped, jumping inside; it was a name high on her list of places to visit, and she knew that it lay on the other side of the Seine and at some distance away.

So she really was being followed . . . She had been followed in Copenhagen and now she was being followed here in Paris. It was actually happening; she could no longer pretend that it was not true, or rationalize it away. *She was being followed*. Her mind reeled at this, and because it was no longer coincidence or supposition or conjecture, it held the shock of finality. She could no longer escape a proven fact or continue to weave deceits: it was actual, it was real. "They're following me, Melissa Aubrey," she whispered, and began to shiver at the horror of it.

"Pardon?" said the cab driver.

She shook her head. They had crossed the Seine and were passing a huge hotel whose sidewalks were filled with café tables under a bright awning. She said suddenly, "I will get out here."

She paid the driver. She was certain the cab had not been followed, but she chose a table beside the street where she could see everyone who passed. Ordering a vermouth from the waiter she lighted a cigarette with shaking hands. She needed people now, she felt tight inside and very frightened; fear always fragmented her and then isolated her and so she sat very still, trying to draw strength from the people around her so that she need not lose the small precarious amount of steadiness remaining in her.

It was Stearns' book that had led her to this. Stearns had been murdered for it, and once it was discovered that he had given the book to her—why, then, she would be murdered, too. *If they put two and two together, if they learn for instance that you also go to Majorca, and that we sat at the same table....* Yet it all seemed so long ago. Time could never be measured by clocks or calendars on a journey like this, and Stearns had happened to her a century ago, before Hamburg, before Copenhagen, but above all before Adam. Since then the meaning and the urgency of Stearns had faded into near-oblivion. She had never wanted to remember him, anyway.

Surely she ought to go to the police now, she thought, but if she could not herself believe in Stearns' reality, would she really be capable of forcing the French police to believe in it? There was nothing provable about the encounter except a book, a worn paperback volume of Emerson's essays that still seemed a joke to her.

Damn Stearns, she thought.

The police would say, "This is very interesting, you traveled aboard a ship with this man, you met him on A deck at ten o'clock during the evening before the ship docked at Cherbourg, and between then and dawn the man was murdered?" They would hold her for questioning, they would ask why she believed she was being followed. Why? Because she had several times seen this man in Copenhagen, she would reply, and now he was here in Paris. Could she prove it was the same man? Only by a man named Adam who might or might not remember The Pale One, and who could be found somewhere in Norway—or was it Sweden or Finland by now? The police could of course contact the Anglo-Majorcan Export Company to ask them if they knew of Stearns, or expected a book of essays, but if Stearns really was a secret agent then it was

possible that his name was not Stearns at all. Besides, she
could herself contact the Anglo-Majorcan Export Company
if she cared to—if she wanted to—if it was important
enough—because in a little more than forty-eight hours
she would be flying to Palma and could discover for herself
if such a company existed.

But at the heart of her dilemma lay the knowledge that
she was as afraid of going to the police as she was of The
Pale One. Jolted, she felt of too little significance to act.
The police were real, and she was not, and if she went to
them she would have to go *now*, today, in a few minutes,
while the implications of The Pale One's presence could be
postponed until she felt stronger. She did not speak French,
she did not know where to find the Seurat or whom to see
there, she was sure that she would be kept waiting and then
treated with hostility. She was far too frightened to con-
vince strangers of her suspicions, she wanted only to find
relief from her terror by obliterating it. A police inquisition
could only bring new stress, and already anxiety was turning her into a cipher.

The waiter brought her vermouth and placed it on the
table. She paid him, hoping he didn't notice her trembling
hands but by now all sense of realness was dropping from
her fragment by fragment. If only she could feel real, if
only Stearns could feel real to her! And Adam, was he also
going to slip away from her into an unfathomable silence
of time, as Stearns had done? When she returned home
would she also have to call him back by conscious and
deliberate invocations of will, by trancelike starings at the
skeletal remains of a rose, by a closing of her eyes to summon back some residual image left behind in the retina?
Her heart ached at this concept of loss. She tried to recall
Adam now, and couldn't, he was absolutely gone, and
tears of grief filled her eyes. There was again nothing solid
or provable to which she could cling, and in panic she
looked out at the people passing by, her eyes imploring just
one of them to bestow upon her a second glance that would
give her back her realness. She found no one, and finding
no one began to take her evil game seriously, to bank her

very existence upon discovering one—just one—whose
gaze would assure her that she was real, that she had substance, that she was sitting here at this café table in Paris.
But although throngs of people streamed past her, their
glances remained fixed upon the street ahead of them, ig-
noring her, or moved with deep interest to the table next to
Melissa.

She turned, curious to see what captured those coveted
glances, and saw that it was not an object or an activity but
a woman, a woman like herself—but much younger, and
very beautiful with the glowing radiance of cared-for
American youth. Everything about her was exquisite: her
long crossed silken legs, her dark suit, the shining blonde
hair, the profile of her flawless face. With a dark flush
burning her cheeks Melissa returned to her drink. Now at
last, in one stroke, she was rendered invisible and there
was no hope at all, but by comparison she felt diminished
and unseen, but above all tired and old. How could she
ever have attracted Adam? Nor could she summon back
Adam's belief in her as a shield now because if Adam
passed today it would be at this gorgeous creature he would
look, not at her. She knew this, and denied even this reassurance—denied every possible reassurance of her existence—Melissa turned upon herself with revulsion and
began plunging knives of hatred into a self that now appeared contemptible and pitiful. As she plunged down into
this spiraling void of nothingness she wanted to cry out
"Adam!" but he was not there, and in his place sat this
woman who was precisely the sort of woman Adam was
accustomed to enjoying—he had said so: poised, sophisticated, knowledgeable. And Adam was above all fastidious:
had it been an absence of such goddesses that led him to
cultivate Melissa instead, who was neither poised, sophisticated nor knowledgeable? Had she been for him in Copenhagen only a compromise, a passing convenience?

She shuddered.

Or would he—and this was the most contemptible
thought of all—would he still choose Melissa because she
was the more available?

She reeled at this insight. Did he—for sport—prefer playing Prince Charming to a Cinderella because it indulged his sense of superiority and flattered his ego? Once she had bravely said to him, "I must be very different from the women you know at home." And he had said nothing, he had not even condescended to deny it.

Once he had said, "I would tell the man to find someone more trusting, more gullible than I . . . Now if he could find someone like *you*—inexperienced, unworldly, and traveling alone—"

Her flush darkened as she stared unseeingly into her drink. It chilled her to realize that anything so real could change like this, it was like holding a many-faceted jewel and by one swift manipulation of the fingers seeing it rendered opaque, dark, and lusterless. "Was it," she wondered unsteadily, "a star-crossed meeting in Copenhagen, or was it a cheap pickup between a man looking for sex and a woman looking for reassurance?"

For looked at now from the estrangement of distance she could see with terrible clarity how vulnerable and how accessible she had been, and this shamed her and distorted everything that she could remember. For a little while she had walked in beauty—but being a man of the world, Adam could have shrewdly suspected that every word was being filed away for later nourishment. It was a form of immortality, wasn't it, to make oneself unforgettable to so many women? Look at the sort of man he was—this she had at least known from the beginning, but in forgiving his vast, perhaps even tawdry, experience with women hadn't she only rationalized away her longing to know him, and could she not, in her need, have been just one more victim of his experience? For when a person's inexperience amounted to a gaping wound, it was difficult to see clearly. A man who lived to please and seduce women was above all an actor whose performance changed with every situation. He could have manipulated her every reaction as adroitly and cleverly as an expert chess player. He could have calculatingly planned every move from the moment that she allowed herself to fall into conversation with him on the tour bus, thinking to himself, "This one will demand special handling. She looks shy, frightened, and unsure of herself, and yet because she is intelligent, I must never be obvious to her."

Her stomach turned at the thought. But he had been traveling alone for six months, had he not? That was a long time, and long enough for the eye to compromise. She remembered him saying, "I should have chosen the other girl on the bus, she would have proven supremely forgettable." That meant that he had been looking for someone, didn't it? She had been flattered by his words when he said them, enjoying the implications of his delight in her, but now she saw their subtler meaning: at the moment when he entered that tour bus almost any woman would have served his purposes.

Now she recalled Adam in detail and literally despised him, for there was no one to tell her who or what he was, and she had met him—been picked up by him, admit it, she reminded herself contemptuously—in a foreign city a continent away from home. Oh yes, he had said lovely things to her, with a deep and obvious sincerity, but he was undoubtedly saying them now to another woman, in another city. She had not mattered to him, she had been only one adventure among many, someone novel and interesting to be sampled, like a new wine, and then forgotten. The humiliating part of it was his success. He had left behind him a shining-eyed little fool. He had mattered *so much*, he'd filled her life—her impoverished, pathetic little life, it seemed to her now—before he passed on to a new game.

Odious . . . and that trick of lighting two cigarettes at once between his lips—she recalled this now and shuddered. That was a trick from an old Charles Boyer movie, wasn't it? It implied tenderness and care—how on earth could she have taken him seriously for even a moment? He was really nothing more than a professional rake except that he operated on a more sophisticated level, adding subtlety, candlelight, and finesse to a tired old game. The flush faded now from her cheeks, replaced by a cold horror at his exploitation, and by her own gullibleness. How ripe she had been—her flesh crawled at the thought, and so great was her feeling of revulsion against herself that she longed to crawl into a dark hole and hide forever. She had never mattered to Adam. The sense of value he had given her had been only a spurious thing, a mockery, a gift lasting scarcely longer than the single red rose he'd given her upon parting—and the rose as well as the sense of value appeared to her now as the most cynical manipulations of all.

God what a fool she'd been.

After a while she scattered a few coins on the table and crept away like the shadow she had become.

The Pale One was stoically waiting for her across the street from her hotel. He did not appear upset by either her disappearance or her reappearance, his glance lifted only once as she walked up the street and then it returned to his newspaper. She did not really exist for him either, she thought bitterly. She existed for no one—not even as a memory—and this was the greatest aloneness of all.

9

She awoke to her second morning in Paris and lay listening to the sounds of the hotel and of the street outside, anchored to her bed by the weight of a terrible inertia. She felt dead inside, killed, destroyed, emptied. Attack with zest? The very words nauseated her when she did not care whether she lived or died. Once—yesterday—she had possessed something, if only an illusion, but then she had turned upon Adam and destroyed him forevermore. It was true that with enormous care she might rebuild what she had leveled, but she no longer trusted herself to do so. For which, now, was the real Adam, the one that she had carried away with her from Copenhagen, or the Adam she had suddenly glimpsed yesterday through a neurotic flood of suspicion and distrust? There was no physical, visible Adam against which to measure memory, and in the seeds of the first Adam—in the ruthlessness she had noted with affection at the time—lay the second Adam of yesterday. It was like Humpty Dumpty, she thought sadly: once broken

he could never be put together again, nor did she have the
energy or the interest to try.

She lay instead in her bed and thought of the day ahead, of
the fifteen or sixteen hours of empty time into which she must
try to breathe life, and she realized now—cynically—the
trap into which she had fallen during those first beautiful
hours in Paris. She had not been self-sustaining after all, she
had been depending upon Adam here just as surely as if he
accompanied her physically. For a little while Adam had
filled her, and then the memory of Adam, but now she was
empty again and so it had been false from the beginning.
Aboard ship she had performed for Doctor Szym, in Copenhagen she had performed for God, and in Paris she had been
performing for Adam. Nothing had changed at all.

She stirred and sighed. She must—had to—keep
going, Pale One or no Pale One. She must carry this leaden
soul around Paris with her and endure its deadness with the
hope that one day the very Time that she berated would
carry her to a new point where life might have meaning
again. But she could think of no reason for leaving her bed:
shops, tours, sightseeing, filled her with distaste, all of
them reflecting back the emptiness within her. She could
feel neither anger nor sadness nor melancholy nor curiosity. She could not feel at all.

She arose and dressed and went downstairs to breakfast.
For a few brief minutes coffee made the world real to her,
but then her cup was empty and still there was nothing real
to do. She asked for another cup, and when the waitress
returned with a steaming carafe there was a man following
her. "This one is Madame Aubrey," the waitress said, and
the man walked over to Melissa's table.

"Mind?" He drew out the chair and sat down across
from her. "Grimes is my name."

She said coldly, "Oh?"

"I've been looking for you."

Melissa said nothing; she felt nothing, not even outrage.

"It's about a man named J.J. Stearns."

She looked at him without interest. "Stearns," she
echoed politely.

"The steamship line gave me your address here," he said softly, watching her sugar her coffee.

She said curtly, "They don't know my address here."

"Yes, they do. They do now. You were questioned by the police in Copenhagen, weren't you? All your addresses were sent back to the steamship office. Now I'm doing a little questioning on my own."

"Are you the police?" she asked bitingly.

"No—no, it's not like that at all. You might say I'm a personal friend of Stearns'. We did the same sort of work." He waited as if he hoped for a reaction from her. When none was forthcoming he added, "If Stearns *did* talk to you at all then you'll know what that means."

Melissa looked at him and said levelly, "This is a very difficult conversation to follow. Did you intend it to be?"

His lips tightened. "Hang it all," he said, and fumbling in his wallet he brought out a card and tossed it on the table beside the croissants. "Here's my identity, look at it, will you? I'm trying to tell you that Stearns worked for your government and mine. Dangerous work."

She had given the card only a cursory glance. "How do you *know* it was dangerous?" she demanded angrily.

He looked suddenly tired. "You don't believe my identity card? Look, do you want a uniform? I don't have a uniform and I don't usually carry a card with me every day saying who I am. It's too risky. Don't you ever take anybody's word for it that they're who they say they are?"

She began to laugh. For a moment she was afraid that she couldn't stop laughing and then a little sob escaped her and she stopped laughing and buried her face in her coffee cup. He had not heard the sob. His brow was all furrows, he was thinking how to reach her, no doubt, how to bring her out from behind the safe high wall she had built around herself.

"I see you don't," he said heavily. "All right, I'll go away in a minute. But Stearns *was* in the employ of our government and he was on his way to Majorca to the NCMC Conference—Conference of Neutral and Committed Mediterranean Countries. It begins in five days in

Palma—several new trade agreements are to be signed—
and what Stearns had uncovered and was bringing to that
conference was going to blow it sky high."

She would not listen to him, she did not want to hear
him. "Go away," she thought stonily, wishing she might
exorcise him.

"That's all anybody knows," he said heavily. "The people I work for believe Stearns' killer got away with what he
was taking to Majorca. I don't think so. I just happen to
feel Stearns was too good, too *damn* good, not to guess
they were onto him and hand his bit of dynamite to someone else." He looked at her. "And you're heading for Majorca and you sat at table 43 with him."

She looked at Grimes, almost wanting to help him. He
sounded so very convincing, so damnably sincere, and yet:
*there may be others after this if they put two and two to-
gether, if they know for instance that you also go to Majorca and we sat at the same table . . .* She remembered that
outside her hotel there lurked a man who had not gotten her
itinerary from the steamship lines or the Danish police but
straight from the source in a little town named Bruxton,
Massachusetts, and he too was there because she was
bound for Majorca and had sat at able 43. If The Pale One
chose to come inside and speak to her would he not be
equally as persuasive and convincing?

She heard herself say in a high, calm voice, "I'm sorry.
I'm going to Majorca, yes, but Stearns gave me nothing. I
scarcely knew the man."

His lips tightened. He picked up the card and placed it
back in his wallet and then looked at her again. "You're
very tense," he said.

She shrugged. "I'm traveling alone. Sometimes it
makes one tense." If he could only *go.*

He stood up and gave her one last thoughtful look.
"Then good luck, Mrs. Aubrey—traveling alone—and
sorry to have bothered you."

"Not at all," she said in her high calm voice, and when
he had left she put down her coffee cup and stood up,
taking great care to remove him at once from her mind so

that she need never remember him. She walked out, carrying her coat, and as she moved up the street she was aware of The Pale One falling into step behind her, but this no longer mattered either, he was only a meaningless appendage, like her shadow.

Doggedly, mechanically, she walked around Paris, staring unseeingly at monuments and buildings. She went to the Louvre and followed a guide through its echoing halls and then she walked to the Jeu de Paume and looked without passion at the Impressionist paintings on the walls. Emerging from its gates she found a café and ordered a sandwich and a glass of wine, and at the far end of the café The Pale One also sat down and ordered with unconscious mimicry. She watched him unfurl a newspaper and hide his face behind it and she thought musingly, "Does he speak French and read it well, or does he use the paper only to conceal himself?" She began to consider the prerequisites of a job like his and to wonder what the rules of surveillance were. If she were accosted by a purse-snatcher on a dark street, for instance, would he come to her assistance? She wondered if in such a situation he would feel obligated to protect her life or if he was awaiting a chance to destroy it. And if murder was on his list she wondered what means he would use to kill her. She was surprised to find that she could consider this with detachment. She tried next to concentrate on him as a person, as a person belonging to her life, since surely she ought to feel less alone in his company, but she could draw no warmth from his presence because it was not in any real sense a presence; he was only there, without communication, personality, or identity. She wondered if he had appreciated or even noticed the Lautrecs at the Jeu de Paume, or the Della Robbias at the Louvre, and then for a reckless moment she thought of walking over to him and saying, "If you plan to kill me, just when will you do it?" But it did not seem worthwhile. She did not feel alive enough to care about death—or was she instead so frightened of death that she could not feel alive? She did not know, she was too apathetic to care.

She stirred and thought, "Oh, why don't I give up and

fly home to Charles?" The thought occurred to her with such savagery that she examined it, noting with clinical interest the lift of relief she could feel at never being alone again, and of escaping this mysterious and formless doom which The Pale One's presence signified. Charles would take her back, Charles would spread great sheltering arms to welcome her, and if those arms were forged of steel, and would presently become chains, was that so great a price to pay for safety when life was such a precarious and dangerous affair? From the seclusion of Charles' arms she could watch life pass by without experiencing it, and if in the end she became a hollow shell what was she now but a shell of fear?

She pushed away the tasteless sandwich and sipped the last of her beaujolais. She saw—as she had always seen, but now with finality—that it was impossible to go back and that it had been too late for a long, long time. Fate, when once it began to move, conspired with Time to slam each door through which one passed, and already change had closed doors and erected walls between her and Charles. Too many words had been hurled like rocks, too many images irrevocably destroyed. She had even crossed an ocean to set foot on a new continent, figuratively as well as literally; and between them now stood Adam— yes, and even Stearns separated them because each had taken her beyond innocence into the holocaust of risk.

The thought carried with it a small sense of relief because it absolved her of choice and brought her closer to acceptance. She came a little to life, and seeing that the waiter had just brought a steaming bowl of soup to The Pale One she arose, scattered change, and walked away, drawing pleasure from this small act of assertion over her shadow as she deprived him of both his lunch and his rest.

Presently, feeling somewhat revived, she even began to forget about him.

The next morning she took a guided tour of Paris and visited Notre Dame and Montmartre but the few English-speaking people on the bus traveled in couples and sounded cross and demanding; in retrospect the tour of Copenhagen seemed to her a singular act of fate for there were no magic people here in Paris, there was no one to rescue her from either her isolation or from The Pale One who followed like a specter. Stoically she crossed Notre Dame and Montmartre off her list, and before she attempted the Eiffel Tower bought a sandwich. Wandering through the Tuileries she came to the sailing pond and sat down on a bench in the sun and unwrapped her lunch. It was peaceful here— water always soothed her. A stiff breeze rippled the pond's surface like crepe, and small boys in short pants chattered and shouted over their sailboats, skating them across the water with shouts of joy and racing to recapture them with boat hooks. The childrens' nurses gossiped in the background under the trees just as they had done when Seurat and Renoir affixed them forever to canvas. Melissa sighed, her sadness a burden today. It seemed that everything numbed her now: Paris, the thought of flying to Majorca tomorrow, the money she was spending on her trip, her aloneness, the obscurity of her future. She could no longer separate her fears or choose one among them to fight, they formed a collective weight that crushed her. But what she really mourned, she knew, was Adam, for in losing him she had lost all hope. It was not that she hoped he might happen to her again, or even someone like him, but rather that with Adam she had dared to trust both herself and life; with Adam she had dared to use all of her faculties, to see and hear and taste and feel again; and now, shaken and lost, she had fallen into muteness, the magic incantations gone. She could not be sorry that once she had sung a song of life, but its echoes barely reached her in this mausoleum she inhabited now. It was hard to see life go, she thought, to feel the stillness return: the stillness not of tranquility but of apathy.

She was scattering the crumbs for the pigeons when she became aware of a woman standing over her and speaking to her in French. Melissa looked up and smiled, grateful to the first person who had spoken to her today. "But I do not understand French," she said. "Do you know English?"

The woman's gestures became more rapid, her eyes narrower, and she held a ticket, pointing to it. Gradually, and in astonishment, Melissa understood what the woman was telling her: it cost money to sit on this bench in the sun, and Melissa must pay her.

Melissa's lips tightened. It was another rebuff. She groped in her purse for fifty centimes, dropped the coin scornfully into the woman's palm and walked away with tears in her eyes.

The tower had remained steadily in front of her for a long time, stabbing the horizon yet seemingly impossible to reach, and then abruptly Melissa came out upon the Avenue de la Bourdonnais and there it was. The Eiffel Tower, she read from her guidebook: 984' high. Open daily from 10:45 to 5:45. Elevator fees: first platform 2 NF; 2nd platform 3 NF; 3rd platform 5 NF. She put her head back and sought the top of the needle-thin spire and it looked high enough to puncture the sun. She winced; heights always made her uneasy, and she realized angrily that the tower was no more than a skeletal framework that irritated space without enclosing it. Her lips thinned. "Well, Melissa?" she demanded coldly, and felt neatly trapped indeed. Because if she ascended the tower it was going to be against all of her instincts and if she did not ascend the tower she would forever know herself a coward. She only wished she had not entered this so casually on her list. Presumably no tourist left Paris without visiting it but she had not stopped to remember that it lacked walls behind which tourists might convalesce from vertigo.

Prodding herself—she had not come this far to be defeated by a blown-up child's erector set, she told herself scornfully—Melissa crossed the avenue and walked up to the ticket window. The first platform, she decided, would not be enough, the highest platform would be too much; she would compromise on the middle one and then come right down again. She pulled out three new francs and purchased her ticket. The elevator was waiting, already half filled with afternoon tourists, among them a number of

American teenagers expressing noisy warnings about jumping.

"Who wants to when we haven't seen the Folies Bergères yet?" demanded one of them, and Melissa smiled faintly.

The elevator came to a creaking halt at the first platform and three women and a man walked out. "I should have gotten off here, too," thought Melissa suddenly, but it was too late. The elevator began its ascent again, and she moved a little closer to the person next to her for consolation, but then abruptly the elevator reached the second platform and stopped.

Melissa drew a deep breath and walked out. Behind her the elevator banged and creaked upward and the squeals of the teenagers grew fainter. She had forgotten there would be a wind up here. It reminded her of the ocean and of the gales that incessantly swept the ship's deck. She walked slowly, cautiously, to the guard rail and halted. The people who had left the elevator with her dispersed to right and left along the platform and presently drifted away. Off to one side she heard the clang of another elevator. "It's going up!" someone shouted in English.

"Good! Let's try the top!"

Melissa remained still. Below stretched Paris, divided from her by space and distance, a diminished and peopleless city like a toy spread under a Christmas tree. She gripped the railing, aware of the hypnotic pull of space. Space frightened her, she supposed that everything without solidity and structure dismayed her: unstructured time, formless days, unenclosed buildings, heights, the sea. But she was here. She was not enjoying herself but she was here on the second platform.

"So now I can go down again," she thought with relief. "Good!" She turned to retrace the few steps she had taken in a direct line from elevator to railing, and her heart gave a sickening leap. A gasp—a whimper—involuntarily escaped her because she had forgotten all about The Pale One. She had neither thought of nor remembered his existence for hours—and he had found her. He was planted squarely between her and the elevator, his eyes resting on her without expression and it was this expressionlessness that added to the horror of the moment for surely there ought to be recognition, she thought—even intimacy—between a stalker and his prey. He had cornered her now. They were utterly alone here in this corner of the platform —one up for him, she thought hysterically.

Here on this windy platform only a railing separated her from Paris below, he need make only one move to close the distance between them and over she would go, plunging down through dizzying space. "Oh God," she thought, "how could I have been such a bloody *fool*!" But it was all over now, everything; she could not move, she only waited, completely paralyzed and submissive, her glance dropping to his tie because she could not bear to look into his eyes and see her death depersonalized and then she could not bear the waiting and she closed her eyes. And still she waited for the feel of his hands on her waist and shoulder, and for the push that would send her hurtling through space into oblivion. They would say she had jumped or fallen and no one would ever know. Time stood still. She waited, drained of life, too weak, too impotent either to move or to cry out, almost longing now for deliverance from the agony of suspense.

The sound of the elevator coming down startled her back to life and she opened her eyes. For a second she did not understand that she was to be reprieved, and then slowly her gaze moved questioningly to The Pale One, and she saw that it was not even a reprieve because he was regarding her with the blank, impersonal boredom of a stranger. It had all been in her mind. Now he detached his glance and turned toward the elevator to enter it and then he stepped back to allow Melissa to enter first, and she was dazed by this polite masquerade when only a moment before—She moved forward obediently. As the elevator descended to the ground floor she felt the shock of the encounter spread through her limbs until, reaching the ground, she tottered from the elevator like an old woman. She moved slowly to a cement pillar and facing it, placed both hands around it for support, heedless of who saw her.

He had not killed her.

*He had not killed her.*

Her lips began to tremble and she placed both hands to her cheeks to conceal them. She realized that someone was asking her if she was all right, and she turned to see a little man with a broom peering short-sightedly up into her face. She nodded and managed a reassuring smile. With enormous effort she pulled herself together and tore herself from the wall to flag down a passing taxi. The man followed and vehemently waved his broom at an empty cab.

"Merci," she told the man gratefully, and he smiled and touched his cap.

She fell into the rear seat of the taxi, directed the driver to her hotel, and leaned back in exhaustion. But now she faced a new terror, because if The Pale One had not killed her—had not even *tried* to kill her—then how much of this did she imagine and how much of it was real? In the darkening cave of her mind it seemed to her that only her death at his hands could have proved her sanity, for if she was in no danger from The Pale One—if she was imagining it all—then she must be slipping into a final madness from which neither Doctor Szym nor God could rescue her.

# 10

SHE COULD NOT GO ON LIKE THIS, THOUGHT MELISSA, NOT
knowing of what and of whom she was frightened. She sat
down at the small writing desk in her room that evening
and put her head into her hands, trying to think, to pierce
the fog of suffocating despair that had enveloped her since
the travel agency's letter had arrived. It seemed to her that
only facts could dispel the mysterious dreads that sur-
rounded her now. After a few moments of quiet she drew
out paper and pen, the typed itinerary, the Carmichael letter, and a calendar.

The air mail letter from the agency was postmarked
June thirtieth Bruxton, Massachusetts. In it Mr. Carmichael referred to a cable received only an hour earlier from
Europe, and a cabled reply that had been dispatched at
once. She circled June 30th on her calendar and concluded
that whoever had demanded her itinerary must have received it—allowing for the time difference—either late in
the evening of June 30th or early on the first of July.

So much for those dates. . . .

She had arrived in Copenhagen on June 29th, late in the afternoon, and had not left her hotel for the rest of the day. She had met Adam on the following afternoon, which was June 30th, the day when the Carmichael Agency in America received the cabled request for her itinerary. It was on the next day, July 1st, that Adam had first pointed out The Pale One to her—and she remembered that she would never have noticed him at all but for Adam's fastidiousness about clothes.

The dates fitted. The Pale One would have had time to receive the cable and pick up her trail at the hotel by that time.

She began examining it next from the other end, from the beginning aboard ship. Stearns had been murdered just before the boat reached its first port, and only a few hours before he was to disembark. What faceless stranger could have poisoned a man already aware that he might be in danger? It scarcely seemed something that a passenger could arrange.

She frowned, trying to fit together the few pieces of the puzzle that she had been given by Stearns and by circumstance. Immediately it struck her as extraordinary that Stearns traveled by sea when a plane would have carried him to Europe so much faster. Such a choice on his part implied an urgent need to deceive, to avoid the predictable and to conceal himself. But in choosing to travel by sea it was also obvious that he had cut himself off from all possible help, for otherwise he would never have had to appeal to a stranger. This in turn implied haste as well as desperation in his selection of routes.

Haste . . . He could have been hotly pursued in New York by enemies. He might even have been discovered in the act of taking something from them, whoever they were, with no time for so much as a telephone call. Perhaps Stearns had jumped aboard ship only seconds before sailing time, believing that he left his pursuers behind, outwitted and frustrated.

But then he really would have been as safe as he felt.

"Unless," she thought slowly, "unless they had someone

already aboard that ship, someone whom they could contact with a description, an explanation, and an order to search and kill. A passenger? No, that would be too wild a coincidence.

"A room steward," she whispered, growing very still. Yes, that would fit. Someone already aboard, placed there long ago for other purposes, such as collecting information. It wouldn't even have had to be Stearns' own room steward so long as there was access to his trays, or his vitamin pills or aspirin.

And Stearns had guessed. Had it been a gaze too frequently encountered for coincidence, a face glimpsed somewhere before, or was it a sensitivity to danger so acutely developed that the scalp prickled and the flesh crawled without tangible provocation?

But his murderer must have been deeply shocked to discover that Stearns no longer carried whatever it was they wanted from him. For five days his murderer must have stalked him, knowing why Stearns was aboard the ship and where he was going, and always supremely confident that Stearns had no knowledge of surveillance. Once this mistake was uncovered, Stearns' murderer must have begun a methodical investigation of everyone with whom the man had contact. When he did this he would come up against the unalterable fact that one other person at table 43 was going to Majorca.

How would he learn this?

"Forms!" she remembered. The forms had been distributed among the passengers very early in the trip. *Name*: Melissa Aubrey. *Travel plans*: Denmark, France, and Majorca. A room steward would have little difficulty in gaining access to such information.

Majorca . . . If they knew Stearns' destination was Majorca, and if they knew or guessed about the Anglo-Majorcan Export Company, then this would label her at once as a possibility. During the twenty-four hours between Cherbourg and Bremerhaven the information could have been sifted, conclusions drawn, and conferences held. And once she had been singled out as the strongest possibility—why, there was the bright label on her suitcase to aid and abet them in gaining even more information.

The Pale One had found her by Tuesday. The Danish police had not found her until Friday of that week.

"They are much cleverer than the police," she thought with a shiver. "But then of course they had the advantage of knowing that Stearns was murdered. Naturally, since it was they who poisoned him!"

Yet if it had taken the police five days to find her, it might not have been easy for *them* to catch up with her. They could have followed her from the ship, of course, or met the boat train at Hamburg. But they might have lost her, as well, and after trudging behind that suitcase with its travel agency label they could have resourcefully sent their cable so that they need never lose her again, and could make efficient arrangements ahead....

But arrangements for what? This was what baffled her, for The Pale One had not killed her after all, and this proved a miscalculation on her part. She began to make a list:

(1) The Pale One does not know that he was a joke between Adam and me in Cophenhagen, or that he was noticed there at all;

(2) He does not know that Joe Carmichael wrote to me about cables and itineraries, or that I am aware that someone cabled for them to America;

(3) He does not (apparently) have orders to kill me;

(4) He has not tried to strike up an acquaintance with me;

(5) No one has even—so far as I know—entered my room or searched my suitcase;

(6) No stranger has tried to speak to me except a CIA agent named Grimes, and he immediately went away (I think) satisfied.

It was all very curious—yet The Pale One continued to follow her every move.

"As if they want only to keep an eye on me," she said aloud, with a frown. "As if they're not sure, perhaps, but are waiting..."

Waiting for what?

They were not threatening her, nor closing in, and apparently they had no intention of hurting her . . . unless?

She drew in her breath sharply. "Unless I arrive in Majorca and head for the Anglo-Majorcan Export Company!" she gasped.

That was it, of course—why hadn't she seen it? She had been so blinded by fear, so afraid of force that she'd not seen that in spite of her traveling alone, in spite of her constant accessibility, The Pale One had remained patiently in the background, no more than a watching shadow. He was there to make certain that she followed the prescribed itinerary, did not fly off to Majorca a day early or make any other unexpected moves.

They did not really know then.

They would not know *unless* she visited the Anglo-Majorcan Export Company. Even in Majorca she would remain safe unless she incriminated herself by going to the Anglo-Majorcan Export Company.

She felt almost dizzy with relief.

She was safe. They did not want her, they wanted only the person who was going to go to the Anglo-Majorcan Export Company.

And that would not be she. Oh, no.

She stood up, excited and dazzled by her conclusions and by the rush of relief that filled her. The life that had appeared so untenable only a few hours ago was now livable and manageable. She discovered that she wanted to live, that she had been *yearning* to live. She began to walk about the tiny room, up and down the aisle between the furniture, and now everything was marvelously real to her again: the room, the sink, the couch, the table, the heavy curtains, the building next door. She touched the wardrobe lovingly. "You're real," she cried with delight. It was glorious to feel alive again after being frightened for days. It was pure joy to relax, to be no longer gripped by terror; she could feel this marvelous sense of reprieve thawing out every knotted tension. Her new life was opening out before her once more; she was not going to be snuffed out after all, she was going to live. She was safe. Not even Majorca held any threat for her now. She could go there tomorrow and fly away again in five days and nothing at all would happen to her, nothing at all—so long as she took pains to go nowhere near the Anglo-Majorcan Export Company. And this she had no intention of doing.

Laughing out of pure relief she began to pack her suitcase for Majorca.

She was at Orly two hours before flight time, as usual afraid—even as she smiled over it—that some unforeseeable circumstance might prevent her reaching the terminal on time, thus condemning her to being left behind and to violating the inviolable order to her itinerary. She could dislike herself for this compelling need to be early yet she could imagine herself waiting until the last minute and jumping into a taxi downtown to say, "Air Terminal please!" and the taxi pulling out into Paris traffic to crash into a second car. What horror to arrive too late and miss her plane!

The fear of missing trains and buses had been a recurring nightmare throughout her life, for was there anything more terrible than the finality of being left behind? Even thinking of it tightened the nerves of her throat. Being too late implied loss, it meant feeling deserted and alone, unprotected and insecure. "Melissa must always be early—hours early!" Charles had been accustomed to saying fondly, as if speaking of a cherishable eccentricity that made her lovable. She tried now to recall that distant Melissa, to picture and to feel the Melissa that had lived with Charles.

She remembered that she had been surprisingly strong and sure as she functioned within her small circle of safety. She supposed that to others she had appeared a veritable fortress of strength, as strong and as composed as the people strolling past her now in this lounge at Orly; and observing them as they smiled, chattered, waved, shouted, and waited, she envied their sureness with passion. To be frightened of many things was a difficult way to live, yet

was she really so different from these people except that
her buried fears had been lifted to consciousness where she
could see and feel and taste them? The fears had always
been there but banished to a depth from which they had
governed her with neither her permission nor her understanding; and from hiding they had ruled her by rendering
flawed judgments and wrong decisions without her awareness of motive or reason. Such people, she reflected, were
the walking wounded of the world, priding themselves on
their health as they rejected responsibility, ran from love,
slapped down minority races, and started wars. Surely it
was better—it had to be better—to begin all over again,
humbly, even if it meant enduring for a while this terrible
defenselessness of healing, this working through the alpha-
bet of fears that had ruled her.

The lounge was filling now with people, among them
The Pale One. She could regard him almost with friendli-
ness today because he had not killed her yesterday; surely
there existed no better grounds for friendship, she thought
with humor, and wondered if she dared to smile at him.
But it was obvious that he had to perpetuate his masquerade and pretend that he had gone unnoticed on the streets
of Paris and unobserved beside the elevator at the Eiffel
Tower. And perhaps it was no masquerade at all, perhaps
he believed in his continuing invisibility.

After a while she moved on to the snack bar for coffee,
and then the gate number was posted and she walked
downstairs to select her seat on the plane. She felt a
woman of the world knowing about such matters now but
still she acknowledged some nervousness over her second
flight and could sense a rising anxiety.

"But after all," she thought contentedly, "in five more
days I'll be back here at Orly again, with Majorca safely
behind me—I'll be waiting for the jet that will take me
home." Home! The word dazzled her. This awareness of
the nearing completion of her journey was one of the rea-
sons for her lightness of heart today; that, and the knowledge that the fears behind her far outweighed any terrors
that could lie ahead. She was delighted to be done with

Paris. She had left Copenhagen—but she was not to think of Copenhagen, she remembered—and presently she would be done with Majorca as well.

"And 'done with' is a horrid way to think of it," she admitted, "but this is because of Stearns." If Stearns had not intruded in her life—and it had really been the worst intrusion possible, coloring the remainder of her trip—it would all have been very different. She remembered that he had warned her—very casually it seemed to her in retrospect—and of course she should have said, "No, thank you." Adam had been quite right about this. But how on earth could she have known what lay ahead? Stearns had startled and then astonished her, and then, abruptly, he was gone. She questioned his moral right—no, really he had none—to involve an innocent woman traveling alone. She could give him the benefit of the doubt and assume that he'd not known the extent of the danger but still it had been extremely reckless and thoughtless of him to approach her. He had been desperate, of course. He had taken a chance on her, knowing very well the odds against his book's ever being delivered. For if he had been murdered then it was because of this book that he'd given to her, and of course he couldn't expect a complete stranger to risk her life, too. In a sense it was his death that absolved her of all responsibility in the matter. World politics did not concern her, the conference in Majorca held no meaning for her, and of course it was her life that was endangered.

Stearns had asked far too much. It had been the rankest imposition on his part to inflict this upon her, but fortunately no one knew that she had the book. If Stearns was dead and she visited Majorca without going anywhere near the export company then no one in the whole world would ever guess that she had carried it off the boat with her. This was important to remember: that no one would ever know. It meant there was no one for whom she had to perform, no invisible audience waiting to applaud her bravery. At the Anglo-Majorcan Export Company they did not even know of her existence, and there was no one capable of proving

that at table 43 Stearns had been anything more than a
dining companion.

Marvelous ... and in five days she would be flying
home. It was a beautiful thing to have the dreads flee, fears
dissolve, and to look ahead to home and to an end of this
unending solitary travel.

"Tickets please," said the smiling young woman.

Melissa climbed on the plane and took her seat, again
over the wing. From here she could see the observation
deck and with surprise she saw The Pale One standing behind the rail, the wind ruffling his hair, his spectacles
glinting in the sun. Yes, it was definitely he, and she realized that he was not accompanying her to Majorca. "We
part company at last," she thought. "How wonderful, what
a relief!" Yet even as the gaiety flared she was aware that
this flight would carry her toward the source of her tension,
closer to the spider's web which she must avoid by a masquerading innocence.

"Good-by, Pale One," she thought as the plane taxied
down the runway—and suddenly with a pang she remembered that it was Adam who had christened him The Pale
One, a beautiful Adam whom she had known long ago in a
fairy tale until he had broken her heart in some way she
could no longer remember.

She leaned forward and fluttered her hand at the faces
lining the observation deck, and as she sank back into her
seat it was to observe with irony that she had been seen off
in at least one air terminal of the world.

# 11

FROM THE MOMENT THAT MELISSA SAW THE ISLAND FROM the air, a green jewel rising out of an infinitely blue Mediterranean, she knew that Majorca was going to be different. Copenhagen and Paris had been gray cities, but this was a country washed by sunlight, wind, and sea. Nor did nearness change this first impression, for as the plane swept down the runway of the airport her glance encountered no towering obstacles of steel but literally rested upon tawny, dust-colored earth, clumps of green and the long shedlike building with corrugated roofs that was Palma's air terminal.

From the taxi that carried her toward Palma she counted seven windmills and was astonished. This was Spain?

"More—many more," said the driver. "All around Palma."

"I didn't know," she confessed.

As they entered the town she thought that this was a place few tourists had discovered, for along the quays fishermen mended their nets, shops were opening after siesta, and the faces in the street were dark, with candlelit eyes. But as they continued along the harbor, leaving the town behind, she saw great tourist hotels edging the Paseo Sagrera and overlooking the harbor, block after block of high white cubes striped with balconies and tiers of awnings.

The taxi drew up to her hotel, swung into its crescent-shaped approach and deposited her at the entrance. She was ushered through glass doors into a huge lobby where every sound was muted and bellhops and desk clerks spoke in quiet, reverent voices. To her left lay a maze of boutiques; to her right, down carpeted steps and through glass doors, she glimpsed a glass-walled dining room with crystal chandeliers and tables piled high with fruit and flowers. Ahead of her, elevators soundlessly deposited tourists dressed for the pool, the tennis court, the cocktail lounge. Only the tourists made noise.

Her room was beautiful, with tiled floor and a balcony overlooking the pool. In the bathroom the water glasses were wrapped in sterile cellophane and the toilet was gift-wrapped in transparent plastic but, ironically, there were smudged footprints on the floor, and Melissa imagined a manager confiding to his maids that sterilizing sufficiently blinded tourists so that dirt *per se* was of little consequence.

Having explored her room Melissa's next act was to open her suitcase and rip a page of blank paper from her sketchbook. On this she drew four large squares, labeling them Thursday—which was tomorrow—Friday, Saturday, and then Sunday. For on Monday she would return to Paris, and then fly home, so that between now and that date stood only four whole graspable days, twenty-four hours in duration, and infinitely manageable at this point with the help of tours, long sunbaths, the selection of souvenirs, visits to Palma, and on Monday the reward of home.

Once the squares were drawn Melissa sat back and looked at them with relief and a deep satisfaction. The mind was a peculiar instrument, she thought as she regarded this handmade calendar, for only a week ago—another Wednesday—she had been in Copenhagen, and a week before that she had been aboard ship, yet if she went back in time to each of those Wednesdays she remembered that Palma had felt to her an insurmountable number of years away. Yet she was here. Time had borne her gently, firmly, and inescapably toward this completion of her trip, and if it had deprived her of Adam, it was also carrying her now toward the possibility of home. It was she who had erected walls of dread around each new country; it was she who had clung to each city, holding back; but Time had only smiled as it swept her relentlessly along.

But still it astonished her to realize that only a week ago she had been in Copenhagen with Adam. It seemed inconceivable to her...a man, a woman meeting. She could almost see them laughing and holding hands in a sunlit corner of her mind but where had they gone? They were no longer together and no longer in Copenhagen; between them already lay Time, and for her the dark days of Paris, yet only seven days ago they had been together and real. She shivered—change again!—and without unpacking her suitcase she extracted from it a sweater and high-heeled pumps, returned her calendar to the sketchbook, zipped and locked her case, and prepared to invade the dining room for dinner.

She dined at eight-fifteen, sweeping grandly into the hall to be seated at a small table beside an enormous window. The maitre d' hovered over her, a boy arrived to fill her water glass, and the wine steward immediately followed. She had the feeling of being extremely mysterious to them, for there were no other women dining alone and this evening she could experience again the sense of freedom that she had begun to feel on her first morning in Copenhagen before she met Adam. Certainly she must be the only other woman traveling alone in Majorca; no one else, she suspected, would be idiotic enough to come by ship and plane to the Balearic Islands when they had all of Europe from which to choose. Tonight she felt distinguished and set apart by this fact, and because she moved with grandness—Majorca was, after all, going to be different—she was aware of people staring at her, and she did not in the least mind because they were looking not at her but at grandeur. Life did have its small moments.

She ordered sangria from the wine steward and shish kebab from the waiter, and as she waited, a woman of the world and with something of Adam resurrected in her, she became aware of one man whose glance did not detach itself from her after the first moment, but who sat and watched her with interest. How perfect, she thought—a man was all that her small triumph had lacked, and when he averted his gaze she frankly glanced at him. He sat with three other people—a man, a woman and a teenaged boy —and it was not difficult to deduce that he was the unattached male of the party. He was deeply tanned, his crew-cut blond hair bleached almost white by the sun, his eyes a blue that contrasted strikingly with the brown of his face and the near-white of his head. She thought he looked like one of those mythical young-old airplane pilots who lived with the elements and whose gaze was accustomed to wind, sea, and great spaces.

He turned again to look at her—it was extremely flattering—and with a faint smile Melissa glanced away. The group arose and made their way slowly out of the dining room, but not before the man had given Melissa a last curious glance. Watching him leave she thought, "Another Adam?"

When she returned to her room an hour later she was humming softly. Flicking on the light she unlocked her suitcase to begin unpacking and at once her humming stopped and she frowned. She had retained a very clear picture of the top layer of her suitcase when she left the room: she had placed the homemade calendar on top of the sketchbook that traveled in the left-hand corner, Emerson's *Essays* had rested beside it, then Henri's *Art Spirit*, two pairs of shoes had lain next to the books, and her plastic traveling case had been wedged into the right-hand corner. Now the flowered traveling case lay in the center with the books on either side of it and upside down, her sketchbook was on the right, and the calendar had been neatly placed on the left, under a pair of shoes.

Her suitcase had been searched.

It jolted her, distracting her at once from happy fantasies of romance. She walked to the door and listened beside it for a moment, and then she went to the window and drew the curtains on the flood-lit pool and the slender moon sailing over the Mediterranean beyond. So they were no longer content to follow at a distance. Had she been wrong—could she have been wrong?—to believe herself safe so long as she went nowhere near the Anglo-Majorcan Export Company?

She sat down on the bed, a little frightened and wary, not quite understanding why they were growing impatient and moving in now. She could not believe that she had deepened their suspicions by coming to Majorca, for if they possessed her itinerary, as obviously they must, they would know that her visit had been planned months ago in America. It had to be that here in Majorca, so near to the point of conclusion, their curiosity and their suspense were growing insupportable. This thought appealed to her, for it made them seem almost human, subject to the same longings for reassurance that she herself experienced. She began to picture someone in Majorca angrily pacing a floor, saying in a harassed voice, "But my God, this is costing us money—two weeks in Copenhagen and Paris and we still aren't sure that she's the right person!" It was soothing to suppose that she might worry *them* a little. Walking over to the suitcase she checked it through again.

But nothing was missing, not even Stearns' book, which at this moment seemed unfortunate to her. "I wish they'd taken you," she told the book bitterly, but not even the most malevolent of glances could exorcise it from sight. Changing into her pajamas she turned off the light and climbed into bed.

Following a ten o'clock breakfast the next morning—she had awaited it impatiently, not yet accustomed to Ma-

jorca's languid pace—Melissa set out to look at the town
of Palma, which she guessed would have little kinship to
the world of tourist hotels. She was quite right. After a
long stroll down the sunny boulevard she turned into the
Plaza Gralmo Franco to meet an older, kinder century.
Here there was deep shade—for only tourists sought the
sun—and a cobbled strip where old men sat and dreamed
and barefooted children played intricate, secret games.
Shops walled in this plaza, but there was not a boutique
among them; they were crammed instead with the staples
of life, and if here and there souvenir merchants had inserted themselves, their shops too had a good-humored
gypsy hawkers' quality. The plaza seemed to Melissa a
picture frame in which an ancient courteous past and an
earthy, practical present mingled, so that it held two dimensions, the one imposed upon the other.

She had carried her sketchbook with her, and she sat
down for a little while on a bench and made quick sketches
of the children and of the iron balconies lining the plaza.
No one objected, and the only attention she drew came
from the warm-eyed young men who distributed their attention equally among all the females. Presently she got up
and left, and passing the post office, telephone company,
and police station headed for the cobbled thoroughfare that
rose steeply toward curving, narrow streets filled with
shops. Here a new century had made inroads, here stood
the shops of leather, glass, fabric, woodcarvings, the windows artfully arranged to catch the eye of the tourist. She
walked from one to another in delight, stopping to examine
delicate carvings of Don Quixote, richly tooled leather
purses, fur rugs, old maps, and jewelry of Spanish gold.

It was some time before she realized that she was being
followed, and then it was due only to a sixth sense that had
begun to appraise coincidences of sound and movement
behind her and to acquire an awareness of footsteps that
halted when she halted, of eyes watching through glass
when she stepped inside a store. It surprised her that her
mind, even as she admired tapestries and old books, could
process the scene around her, assessing and timing and

drawing significant conclusions like a computer. Two pairs of footsteps, two pairs of eyes, whispered this sixth sense, warning her, but both feet and eyes remained elusive, always just around a corner although once, turning very quickly, she saw two men disappear much too hastily into a shop. They wore black suits and cocoa straw hats, and she thought they appeared to be young men. Their presence made her aware of the fact that she had wandered quite far from the Gralmo Franco, and that each shop she entered carried her deeper into this maze of slanting, cobbled alleys and squares. Her map gave no names but it did assure her that this network of streets was only several blocks deep and wide and this tempered her uneasiness so that before retracing her steps she calmly stopped to buy a few woodcarvings.

On the way back her shadows remained unseen, but when she passed a man in a black suit fanning his face with a cocoa straw hat she thought he might be one of them. She came upon him suddenly and he at once glanced away, which set him apart from every native male she had encountered in Palma. He was not young, though, and his face was thin and ferretlike.

Presently as she continued to follow the twists and turns downhill she came out upon a street she had not seen before. This one was broad enough for cars and its shops had a settled, businesslike appearance foreign to the tourist trade. At this end of the street a stone well was set into the pavement, with steps surrounding it. It looked such a pleasant neighborhood that Melissa decided to follow the street to the end. She took a step forward and then stopped as a harsh, urgent shout from down the street broke the quiet, and behind her she heard footsteps break into a run on the cobbles. Her glance swerved to the man who had shouted. She saw him standing at the next corner staring in her direction with his mouth open. She turned to look at whom he shouted and saw a man running toward her down the alley she had just left. When he saw her he stopped running and slowed to a self-conscious walk, and suddenly, jarringly, Melissa realized that both of these men wore black suits and cocoa straw hats and that the shout and the running steps concerned her, that for some unknown reason she had upset the two men so that she was the object of this sudden tension that ripped apart the tranquility of this street. Across the road a man and woman had felt it, too. They stopped laughing, their mouths still open in surprise at the strident shout, and an old woman seated on the steps of the well gaped at Melissa. The entire block had become abruptly, ominously still, as if life was held momentarily in suspension. An indefinable menace hung in the air, completely puzzling to Melissa until she looked again to the man who had shouted and her glance fell by accident upon the sign posted on the nearest building. This was the Veri Rosario.

Slowly, almost stupidly, her gaze moved along the signs hanging the length of the street and there it was, like something experienced in old nightmares, a small white sign with black letters announcing the Anglo-Majorcan Export Company. Something like a long sigh escaped Melissa and then—calmly ending the moment of suspension she moved forward and without hesitation crossed the street to enter an alley that would remove her forever from the Veri Rosario. No more than a moment had passed since the man had shouted. She must have jolted him into betraying himself, or perhaps he had called to his comrade for help.

It was like being wrenched out of a deep sleep and Melissa was trembling as she came out upon the Plaza Gralmo Franco. It was not her carelessness that shook her, although she found it unforgivable, but rather it was the sensation of having stumbled to the edge of an abyss, of having looked briefly into a world of violence where no laws were recognized and no mercy discernible. *What would have happened if she had continued her stroll down the Veri Rosario?* She could not easily shrug away the abrupt urgent shout of the one man, the running footsteps of the other, or the resultant sense of nightmare. It had been like a slow-motion moving picture suddenly shifted into high speed; the one moment everything calm, the scene a cobbled

street peopled with browsing tourists, and then the menac-
ing shout.

But even more sobering was the realization that she had
seen the Anglo-Majorcan Export Company with her own
eyes for this gave it a reality that it had never possessed for
her before. She knew now that it existed, and that behind
its façade there might even be real people who mourned
Stearns' death. The reactions of the two men following her
had verified the significance of the shop, thus adding another dimension of identity to its existence and marking it a
place of danger. Because it was no longer just a name to
her now, because she had seen it and it was a provable
reality, she found herself recalling Stearns with astonishing
clarity. She was able even to remember the texture of his
voice as he gave her the book on A deck.

This incident on the Veri Rosario upset her. She realized
that it had undermined something that she could not afford
to lose, it was challenging her to acknowledge something
unacknowledgeable. She felt obscurely oppressed as she
walked up the plaza, as if she had acquired a burden of
which she must rid herself. She found herself passing the
police station, the telephone company, and the post office
again, and on impulse—thoroughly disoriented—she
mounted the stairs of the telephone company and walked
inside. She had taken only a few steps into its dim interior
when a man asked her in English what she desired. "I'd
like a telephone number," she told him.

"But of course, let me be of service. What is the name
of the people to which you speak?"

Out on the steps she saw a man in a black suit loitering,
and realized what a fool she was. "Excuse me—gracias,"
she stammered, and turned and walked out, appalled at her
folly. In another second she would have requested the telephone number of the Anglo-Majorcan Export Company
and her words would have been irretrievably spoken aloud,
they would have become available to any man who wished
to know what the American señora had wanted and a link
would have been forged between her and Stearns and the

export company. She might just as well have walked down
the Veri Rosario and entered the building. She shuddered.
She had come to Majorca to display her innocence and in
one hasty moment she had very nearly thrown everything
away, perhaps even her life. Nor could she chance using
the telephone at the hotel, either, for again there might be a
man in a black suit who checked such requests. She must
—had to—remember that she was to leave Palma on
Monday without giving away any knowledge of the export
company, and certainly without succumbing to any quixo-
tic impulses.

The hotel was now the only safe place for her in an
unsafe world, and as she hurried toward it up the boulevard
she could regard with satisfaction what she had earlier
scorned. Having discovered that she could not trust herself
she must place all of her trust in this monument to security
instead. It was why the hotel had been built, of course: to
please and to reassure tourists who wanted no undermining
influences from the world outside its walls. Here lay the
ultimate safety of all, the safety of the womb, and she
could appreciate this fact as never before, she could appreciate the young men of the island who wore the insignia of
the hotel because they had been civilized and motivated, in
fact everything in this particular corner of Palma had been
sterilized and made palatable. How peculiar that she had
not understood this, but had scoffed at travelers who must
arrive in a country only to ignore it and hug the pools, the
dining rooms, the boutiques. She too would ignore Palma
now.

She walked up to her room and changed into her bathing
suit, gathered up robe, cap, purse, sketchbook, and towel,
and returned to the lobby. There was a line at the tour desk
and she inquired the reason of the desk clerk. "It's the
Caves of Drach tour tomorrow," he explained. "You don't
know of it? It is very popular, an all-day tour made only
twice a week. Very fine, you should see it."

"Obviously I should," said Melissa firmly, and she
joined the line and paid for a reservation. She was done

now with unguided and misguided ventures into the unknown, it was time to join such well-organized rituals of her own people, the tourists. With her next day competently arranged she went to the pool and captured a chaise lounge in the sun. . . .

# 12

SHE DINED ALONE THAT EVENING, SITTING STRAIGHT AND proud beside the window because she was aware of The Profile's gaze upon her just as it had followed her all afternoon at poolside. "I have an audience again," she told herself. "I can sit here proudly because there is again someone for whom to perform." She had arrived later than the man, who was dining tonight with the teen-aged boy. When he arose to leave she was not at all surprised to see him go out of his way to pass her table. Nor was she surprised when he paused beside her and waited for her to look up.

He said with a slow smile, "I think you're American, too."

"Yes, I am," she said brightly. "From Massachusetts. And you?"

"From California." He held out his hand. "Marc West's the name."

She shook his hand. "How do you do, and I'm Mrs. Aubrey. Melissa Aubrey."

He said gravely. "I was wondering if you'd care to join

me later in touring some of the nightspots here."

"But I'd be delighted," she told him with equal gravity.
"Is that your son traveling with you?"

"I'm not married," he said. "No, that's Peter Carmer.
His parents are still at the pool." He added politely but
with infinite meaning, "And you are traveling alone, too,
Mrs. Aubrey?"

"Yes, quite alone."

"Fine!" His smile registered his pleasure. "Shall we
meet then at nine in the lobby?"

"At nine—and thank you," she said. Still smiling she
watched his broad shoulders move across the room to join
the waiting boy. So it had happened, she mused; incredible! Life did have magic still, and she and Marc West
would see Palma at night and softly, gently come to know
each other . . . it was all so smooth, so effortless, the way
inevitable things *must* happen.

She dressed ritualistically in her most striking frock,
like a person whose life might be forever changed in the
course of the next hours. "I need an evening like this," she
thought. "I need it and I deserve it, I've handled all this by
myself for much too long, and now it's time to confide in
someone." The thought of sharing her burden gave a feeling of joy. To tell someone of what she had endured, to
relinquish decision, to hear a man say with authority, "Let
me take care of everything, I'll see that this shocking affair
is brought to an end at once." Later she would tell him that
in her mind she had called him The Profile before she
knew his name, and he would say, "For me it was seeing
you arrive in the dining room that first evening, you looked
so superbly fearless as you sat there alone . . ."

Promptly at nine o'clock Melissa descended in the elevator to find Marc West waiting for her near the first of the
boutique shops. He was in conversation with a middle-
aged couple, each of them plump-breasted and very American, the man in a white dinner jacket, the woman in a
wildly flowered dress. Seeing Melissa Marc West smiled.
"Here she is," he said. "This is Mrs. Aubrey, folks. Mrs.

Aubrey, I'd like you to meet the Jamisons, Joe and Hazel."

"How do you do."

"Isn't Majorca divine?" beamed Hazel.

Melissa nodded with enthusiasm. "Yes." She smiled at
Marc, waiting for him to disengage them tactfully from the
Jamisons, but his eyes were intently fixed upon two people
crossing the lobby. "Emil," he called, "Emil, you and
Betty care to join our group tonight?"

Melissa was surprised. She glanced at the Jamisons,
both of whom smiled eagerly back at her with very white,
square teeth. She realized in astonishment that the Jamisons were also going to view the night life of Palma with
Marc West, and that in all probability Emil and Betty
would be joining them, too. She felt not so much disappointed as wary; she had not expected so pedestrian an
arrangement from a man who looked as Marc West did. It
was no longer a question of romance but of taste.

She realized that she had just been introduced to Emil
and Betty Carmer, who were Peter's parents, and that they
too were smiling at her expectantly. "You the lady artist?"
asked Emil brightly.

Marc West laughed. "Yes, we've all been curious. Are
you?"

Melissa nodded, and Emil crowed triumphantly.
"Thought so."

Marc West said gravely, "We saw you sketching at the
pool this afternoon. That's what I said right away, remember, Emil? I said 'You can tell by the way she looks
that she's some kind of artist.'"

"But how thrilling," said Hazel.

Emil's wife said, "Do you make ashtrays?"

"I make pictures," said Melissa, bewildered. "That is, I
paint pictures."

"Do any nudes?" asked Emil with a wink.

Hazel poked him in the ribs. "Now don't you go getting
ideas there, Emil. Betty, you'd better watch him tonight.
Marc, what are we waiting for?"

"I had hoped the Robertsons would join us," he said,

plainly disappointed. "But obviously they're still tied up. Shall we find a taxi?"

He grasped Melissa's arm. As they moved toward the doors he said, "The Robertsons' daughter flew in unexpectedly today but there's not a room available in Palma. At last report the manager was trying to find a cot for her. It's because of the conference beginning here soon," he explained. "Political conference."

"Uh—yes, I've heard about it," she said politely.

Two taxis were ordered and Marc West handed her into one. Behind them Hazel erupted with shrill laughter at being told she must sit on her husband's lap in the second cab, and Melissa thought, "But this is deadly, why does he tolerate these people?" Catching his glance she smiled faintly but his eyes held no hint of conspiracy. "This is a good group we've got tonight, don't you think so, Mrs. Aubrey?" he said, smiling.

She was startled. "Group?" she murmured dazedly.

"We had a good group last night, too," he said. "You'd be surprised how many Americans are here, Mrs. Aubrey."

Melissa said weakly, "I already am."

There was a long silence as the taxi pulled away from the hotel. Marc West ended it at last by saying, "Yes, sir, we're all lucky to have a roof over our heads. How long ago did you make *your* reservation here, Mrs. Aubrey?"

"Last April, I believe."

"And did you come over by ship or plane?"

"Ship," she said, and then, politely, "And you?"

"Plane."

Another silence followed, and Melissa discovered that she could think of absolutely no way to keep the conversation moving. "And for how long are you traveling?" she asked desperately.

"I'm only here for a few days," he said. "Then back to the old salt mines."

She winced at his clichés. "And for you what are the salt mines?" she asked.

He laughed. "Now that's what I like to forget while I'm on vacation. And in a place like Majorca I can."

She discovered that she did not in the least care, but that it closed still another avenue of conversation. They were suddenly rescued, however: lights bathed the interior of the taxi, it drew to a halt and they had arrived at another hotel. They walked through a palm-studded lobby very similar to the one they had just left and then into a dim room containing more palms, an orchestra, and small tables. Hazel was already directing a waiter in the grouping of several small tables together. "Isn't this place darling?" asked Hazel, glancing up with a smile.

"Darling," echoed Melissa in a depressed voice.

They sat down and ordered drinks and Emil at once told a very bad joke. Marc West laughed hilariously, and Melissa turned to look at him. He was such a—a ponderous man, she thought, his personality so completely at odds with his handsome, even romantic appearance. Joe Jamison was now taking his turn at an equally poor joke and she thought grimly, "I don't think I can stand a great deal of this." She glanced at the two women and they each smiled at her eagerly. "Let's order another round of drinks," suggested Hazel, beaming.

Melissa thought, "Who am I trying to please, why am I smiling eagerly, too?" Already the muscles of her cheeks quivered from the fatigue of pretending. Feelings of entrapment added to her weariness. She reminded herself that if she left now she would be inexcusably rude, but the thought of remaining with them, of submerging her own self in an effort to act interested and even civilized, utterly dispirited her. Suddenly and firmly she pushed back her chair. "I'm sorry," she said aloud, and then lifting her voice, "I'm sorry but I've just remembered that if this is Thursday then I must be back at the hotel for a phone call at ten o'clock."

Five pairs of eyes swiveled toward her in astonishment. "A phone call here—in Europe?" Emil asked skeptically.

"From Paris," lied Melissa flatly.

Marc West said smoothly, gravely, "Then allow me to take you back, I'll wait with you for your call and bring you back here again."

But Melissa was already standing and poised for flight. "I think it would be better if you didn't, it's an extremely *personal* telephone call."

Marc West looked taken aback and then incredulous, but she did not wait to observe any further reactions. "Delighted to have met you all!" she cried, suddenly gay now that she was to leave their suffocating company. With a wave of her hand she turned on her heel and fled.

Once she had regained her room Melissa began to laugh. "'Won't you join our group?'" she repeated, locking the door and tossing the key on the bed. "'Don't you think we have a good group tonight, Mrs. Aubrey? We had a good group last night, too.'" But her laughter quickly subsided for she was not really amused by the incident. The man struck her as tragic who must collect people, the more the better, in order to defend himself against experience. She felt cheated instead: all the ingredients of magic had been there, the whole encounter had possessed every quality of a fairy tale, the exchanged glances, the idyllic atmosphere all leading up to the confrontation and the invitation to Melissa to join him for the evening—and then it had proved revolting. "Adam has spoiled me," she thought, and then she realized, "No, it is not only Adam, it is myself, too."

She stopped pacing, surprised by this thought, and suddenly she realized the extent of the change inside of her. She had lost something that had been an integral part of her for years, but what she had in truth lost—she saw this now—was the sickest part of all: she could no longer weave images or distort what she saw. Her needs were being replaced by values so that in her very failure tonight there was success. The knowledge transfixed her, and she stood unmoving as she sought to understand it. For she would have liked to change Marc West into a man of integrity. She once might have willed him to be everything that she wanted—another, more possessable Adam—but she could no longer accomplish this. Try as she might, the man remained what he was: empty, unaware, and vain. This time not even her need to escape herself could carry her past reality. She could not construct a glorious phantom even of a man who was handsome, available, and attentive, because in spite of being all of these he was without a soul. He was literally, uninhabited.

She turned off the lights and sat down on the bed, thinking of this in the darkness as she listened to the sounds of music in the hotel below. She felt alternately frightened and intoxicated by this new freedom, a little dizzied by the vision it gave her of a life governed by choice rather than compulsive need. She found herself smiling at the audacity of her flight from the very epitome of everything once desirable to her, above all her flight from the available. When she fell asleep she was smiling.

# 13

But in the morning it was different. She awoke with a deep sadness in her and an edgy sense of restlessness, for she had lost something again. She wanted to turn back—now, quickly, before it was too late—and recapture that outgrown self for there was nothing yet to take its place. She was not ready for this new, discriminating Melissa, for to be discriminating was to remain alone, and she did not want to be alone. Once again she felt suspended between two points, neither here nor there.

As she dressed for the Caves of Drach tour, she wondered despairingly, "To whom can I turn now?" But again there was no one, and in this restlessness there was the feeling that she moved nearer and nearer to some discovery that she scarcely dared make, as if last night had carried her to the brink of something new and momentous which she could not bear to experience lest it shatter her.

She had an early breakfast and was one of the first to board the waiting tour bus. After an exchange of pleasantries with the driver she found a seat in the center next to a window. She was not really surprised when one of the men, in a black suit, climbed aboard the bus; he did not give her so much as a glance but looked grave and pre-occupied as he moved to a rear seat. Next, to her surprise, came Marc West carrying several cameras slung around his neck but he was followed—mercifully—by the Carmer boy. They chose the two seats in front of her.

"Hi," said the Carmer boy, grinning.

"Good morning," said Marc West stiffly.

She nodded, and amused herself by glancing over the brochure in her lap. She saw that they would visit the Caves of Drach, a pearl factory in Manacor, the Caves de Arta, and if they wished they might swim in the Mediterra-nean during the tour's mid-afternoon siesta. It sounded pleasant but for her its major contribution was the filling of eleven hours and the cancellation of another day on her calendar. For there were to be no magic rescues on this strange odyssey of hers, she understood this now with a certain grimness. She had begun her trip alone, and must end it alone, with a few interesting memories but nothing more. Understanding this, that the trip was not to solve any problems at all, it held very little interest for her any longer, she was only impatient to end it. "Only two and a half more days," she remembered, "and then I can go home knowing that I followed the itinerary to the bitter end."

Presently the bus moved on to another hotel, and then it left the town behind and moved out across a countryside almost Biblical in texture with warm dusty earth, groves of olive trees, narrow winding roads, and sleepy vineyards. After an hour of patient, leaden observing, Melissa dozed. She awoke with a start to see that they were entering the plaza of a small town. Marc West turned and said politely, "You have been asleep."

"Yes," she admitted.

"We are about to visit the Caves of Drach."

"Oh—thank you," she said, but he had already turned back to his cameras, which he was loading with film.

The bus stopped and the driver sprang from his seat, a

round jovial little man with sparkling eyes. "But now we are here," he said happily, "and you will see—the Caves of the Dragon! Explored and opened up by the French, as you will discover from many of the names given the points of interest. The Majorcan people are quite bored by their caves—after all, they have them! It is you outsiders who discover them to be—beautiful! Unique! Entirely enchanting! Where nothing, nothing at all, is what it appears to be! Shall we go, ladies and gentlemen?"

Melissa felt a quickening of interest. Perhaps here, perhaps today, she would find the capacity to enjoy again. Marc West stepped back to let her precede him, and as they moved out into the sunshine, she realized that he had subtly maneuvered her into joining him and the Carmer boy. Did he so badly need reassurance after her rude behavior last night? she wondered. Knowing that she disliked him, as she did, was he now going to insist upon charming her into liking him? It was a dismal thought. They moved in a group down pebbled paths toward the caves' entrance. Melissa said to Peter with a smile, "Excited?"

He grinned. "Oh, well—you know." He was looking at the postcards and souvenirs inside the tent at the entrance. "Hey, Marc, there are things for sale!"

"Buy anything you'd like," said Marc West but he remained, perversely, beside Melissa. "Did your phone call from Paris come through all right?" he inquired suspiciously.

"Yes, it did, thank you," she lied. In turn she was tempted to ask if he thought they traveled with a good group today—her edginess felt very near to hostility. Instead she moved a little away from him.

Their guide was summoning them. "Ladies and gentlemen," he said. "Enough postcards have been sold to you now by my relatives so that we may begin the tour. Shall we go?"

On this small joke they entered the cave by means of a ramp that took them down into the underground. As they left daylight behind to wind their way into the first well-lighted chamber, their guide began a recitation of facts in a mock-serious voice.

"The entire cave," he was saying, "is a grotto of some 2200 yards of total length and divided into four branches, the White Cave, the Black Cave, the Cave of Louis-Salvatore, and the Cave of the French. The incomparable beauty of its formations, the greatness of the Lake of Miramar, and the number and clearness of the other lakes, make the Drach one of the most beautiful caves in Europe." More casually he added, "Now we go through a grove of palm trees, eh? You Americans can pretend you are in your state of Florida."

They had entered a world of surrealistic shapes and fantasies, where illusion had become reality. Yet it was not frightening: Melissa felt like Gretel walking into her gingerbread cottage. The palm trees were perfectly formed, but formed entirely of rock, and now they were passing among giant mushrooms. In a corner along one wall stood a waterfall, frozen in the act of descent, and overhead the ceiling dripped with stalactitic lace. It was a madness so harlequinesque that it struck an answering cloud in Melissa and filled her with laughter. For nothing here was as it appeared to be; everything was almost but not quite real, so that it had the effect of making her feel irrepressibly sane.

"Presently," continued the guide, "you will see our first lake, the water of which is slightly salt. The water in the lake undergoes a slight fall or rise of a few inches according to the level of the Mediterranean, its winds, its storms. You may observe the sediment marking the highest level of the waters. This is, as you see, a marine grotto but of an exceptional extension."

They moved through exquisitely wrought pillars to pass into a broad amphitheater, and there was the lake—except that it couldn't possibly be a lake, thought Melissa, it could not be anything but a mirror for it was utterly still and mute, like glass. She paused to watch it disbelievingly. It did not move; nothing moved. In its transparent depths the reflection of the cave's ceiling eerily mingled with the rocks and reefs lying on the floor of the cave, and their mingling created dizzying and baffling illusions of space and content. She lifted her eyes. Across the still lake a scarlet light illuminated a cove, and in the twilight just beyond the light Melissa saw the silhouette of a devil frenziedly dancing on a rock. In another corner a great, sinister finger pointed to the sky. She shivered at the stillness of so much vitality frozen into rock. Realizing that she was becoming a straggler she began to walk quickly toward the others.

Marc West was kneeling on the path ahead of her taking another photograph—his flashbulbs had already grown tiresome—and as she drew near him he stood up slowly, his bulk blocking the narrow path. "Mrs. Aubrey—"

She glanced ahead. The others were just disappearing in the next chamber. She said, "The tour—"

"Mrs. Aubrey, I'd like to speak to you a minute."

"I'm certainly *here*," she reminded him pointedly but he did not take the hint and move. They were now quite alone in the amphitheater, on the path that rimmed the lake. It was curious how empty, how devoid of human life these stone walls felt suddenly. "What is it?" she asked impatiently. "We're losing the others."

"I seem to have been very clumsy," he said. "There wasn't any telephone call for you from Paris last night. You didn't even expect one, did you?"

Jarred, Melissa said breathlessly, "I don't see what business it can possibly be of yours, Mr. West," and then, aware that she was alone with this man who was blocking her path she added quickly, "Please. Surely we can talk about this as we walk along, Mr. West. We're losing the tour!"

"You're frightened," he said. "I don't understand why I've frightened you."

"How can it matter?" she demanded fiercely.

He said heavily, "It matters because you knew Stearns."

The name came as a blow. She recoiled, shocked beyond comprehension at hearing Stearns' name spoken here, and by this man. Stearns again. It was unbelievable.

"Here," he said, slipping a card from his camera case. "I'm a United States agent, Central Intelligence."

Her gaze obediently fell to the card but once she had seen it she was only the more wary and shaken. He could not know that only a few days earlier a similar card had been dropped in front of her beside a tray of croissants in a dining alcove in Paris. Her artist's eye had retained the impression of what she had seen then, and now it noted the differences in this card of spacing, print, and composition —the card was the crudest of forgeries. "Who are you?" she gasped, one hand going to her throat. He only pushed the card close to her face, blinding her with it until it became an instrument of menace.

"Didn't you?" he demanded. "Didn't -you know Stearns?"

"No," she whispered, and the silence following her whisper was more deafening than the panic screaming inside of her. Now there was menace even in the rocks surrounding her for they were dead, inert, centuries old, and oppressive. The lake beyond Marc West remained still and dead, lacking current or movement, and out beyond the lights the devil still danced, suspended forever in his doomed and mirthless pose. In this silent world of distortion where rocks masqueraded as trees and devils and flowers, it struck her that Marc West was the most grotesque masquerade of all. She had believed him harmless, even a bore, and now she was sick with horror at what he must be.

He was saying, "You traveled on the same ship with him, you sat at the same table with him, you can't have forgotten him. Stearns, a man with blue eyes—"

"No," she cried desperately, and, absurdly, there slipped into her mind a phrase from the Bible, *The cock shall not crow til thou hast denied me thrice*. She bit her lip. "There was a man by that name aboard ship, but I didn't *know* him. Now please—"

He moved closer as if he must forcibly wring from her something more. His eyes frightened her and she edged back among the rocks until she met a wall of stone and there was no further retreat for her. "You fool," he said furiously, "don't you understand this is no tea party you're mixed up with? Don't you know what the stakes are? This is *government* business. You must have more to tell me, admit it—you did know him!"

His hands came up to seize her shoulders—was he going to shake her or to strangle her? She screamed, and ducking her head she slipped under his lifted arms. He spun and grabbed her, catching one shoulder. With a little sob she fell to her hands and knees, loosening his hold until she had escaped his hands. Then she was on her feet and running—back and away, in the direction in which the tour had begun. Behind her Marc West shouted, "Trust me! You must trust me!"

Up steps and down she raced, frantic now to get out, to reach the entrance of the caves. For a little while she heard Marc West behind her, heard him swear once as he slipped on a stair. She only continued her blind rush to the sunlight, longing for release from this hideous fairyland of rocks under the earth.

The sunlight nearly blinded her. She stopped and put a hand to her eyes and the man at the postcard stand said, "But madam, you must go back, this is not the exit!" She gave him a blank look and began to run again. It was like emerging from a dark nightmare. Her toes churned up the pebbled path as she raced toward the plaza. There was a taxi there.

Running across the square she reached the driver to say breathlessly, "Please—can you take me to Palma?"

He looked at her drowsily. "Palma! But this is—" He shrugged helplessly, making a sign of long miles.

She tore open the door of his car and sat down. "I'll pay you," she said. "Whatever it comes to, what does it matter? I can pay you." She brought out travelers' checks and flashed them in his face. "Palma," she said flatly. "Palma, *please*."

He shrugged and turned back to his wheel. "Okay, Palma," he said, and with a grinding of gears they moved off.

# 14

She huddled in the rear seat of the taxi, unspeakably drained and tired. It seemed to her that she had been running for a long, long time, that she had been running forever, until the disease had spread to her spirit. "That man was frightening, terrible," she thought, but the fact that she had escaped him seemed of small importance at the moment. She thought wearily, "It's like a hall of mirrors, and into every mirror I look I find Stearns."

She realized that she must get out of Majorca—at once, even today. A plane for Paris left Palma each afternoon at four, and she could see no reason why today's flight would not have room for one more person. It was the incoming flights that were difficult, because of the Conference.

The Conference . . . she shivered. "It's I they're looking for," and then, "Did Stearns really expect me to deliver his book?"

The thought had slipped unbidden into her mind and she recoiled violently from it. "Preposterous—madness," she thought, and then, tentatively, "He had no right..." and then, "Dear God, I *can't*."

Beyond the glass window the sky was a glorious shade of blue and when they met another car on the narrow winding road there was a joyous exchange of horns blowing and voices shouting, but Melissa remained walled off from the world, literally shielded behind glass. Her panic had left her but as it receded it only uncovered the deeper undercurrent of defeat with which she had begun her day. Now Marc West had badly frightened her, adding exhaustion.

She knew that some decision was necessary now, that she must no longer drift with the tide of her rigidly defined itinerary, yet any course that she might take implied decision and action, and she felt capable of neither. The thought of remaining in Majorca for two more days was as intolerable as the thought of leaving it today. She could not decide whether to go or to stay. She could only whisper over and over again, "I didn't ask for this, why has it happened to me? Why?"

It seemed to her at this moment that she had reached the end, and that in reaching the end she had, paradoxically, returned to the beginning, for she was once again incapacitated by conflict. She had never escaped her doom, she thought bitterly, her odyssey had been only one more blind and compulsive flight from reality. She could not change. She had never been anything but a mechanical toy that Dr. Szym had wound up and directed upon its way, but now the momentum had spent itself and the winding mechanism was running down. She had succeeded neither in finding herself nor in losing herself. All her past hopes appeared to her now as totally meaningless and monstrously pathetic.

"One rose," Adam had said. "It will stay fresh until you too leave Copenhagen..."

"It's an extremely valuable package," Stearns had said. "Quite small. It's a book."

They were entering the environs of Palma now, and suddenly Melissa could no longer bear her thoughts, she must walk the rest of the way. It was barely noon, there was still time to think. To the driver she said, "Stop at that bank over there, will you?" She held up the travelers' checks as explanation and he pulled in beside the curb. She went in and cashed several checks and returned to stuff pesetas into the man's fist. "Thank you," she said. "I'll walk the rest of the way. Gracias."

He drove away smiling. Across the street she saw a familiar man in a black suit step out of a car and she thought wearily, "Oh damn, now it begins again." They would have telephoned from the caves, of course, and the others would have begun watching the roads into Palma. She felt stifled and confined, and she began to walk very quickly, aware of her wasted day, aware of the eleven carefully planned hours which she had destroyed by flight. She realized that her edginess had been deepened by the long ride back to Palma but it was more than a succession of small defeats that troubled her.

"I'm a coward," she thought, naming it. "But I've always been a coward and now I'm tired to death of pretending I'm not. All I want is to go *home*."

Yet even the thought of home did not unburden her. The weight of restlessness persisted, the feeling of something undone, something lost that prevented rest. She felt that if only she could discover what it was then she might discover joy again, and be at peace with herself. Marc West had frightened her but she knew that he was not the source of her defeat: this same feeling had been a companion when she climbed aboard the tour bus that morning.

"Silly, childish Melissa," she whispered, her anger returning. "You're in flight again—but damn it, from whom are you running?"

She increased her pace, as if by walking very quickly she might gain the illusion of going somewhere—her whole being demanded haste to dissipate the rising tide of anger at herself. She walked up and down streets aimlessly until, tiring, she resorted to dreary wandering. She saw nothing and heard nothing and this too was waste. Deep inside of her the dialogue continued: "You left the ship in a state of trauma, Melissa, and then you left Copenhagen numb with fear at your first plane flight, and in Paris you were so terrified that you did nothing but creep about . . . is this living?"

"That's unfair," retorted her other self. "For see how brave you've been to come this far—and alone, too—and it is absolutely no fault of yours, Melissa. This trip would have been delightful if that horrid man Stearns had never intruded."

"Oh come now, you're feeling sorry for yourself. Are you really that heroic? Blame it on Stearns if you must, but on the subject of Stearns why should he bother you? You've done a very successful job of forgetting him, haven't you?"

She began to walk faster, to escape both her thoughts and the confusion of conflict. She reminded herself that in only a matter of hours she could be on the plane leaving Majorca for Paris. Once on that plane, knowing that she was on her way home, she could relax at last. Oh the beautiful safety of home, she thought longingly; once she reached it she would never, never—

She stopped walking. The rest was implied: once at home she would never leave it again . . .

"The circle of safety and ease," she thought despairingly. She had not, after all, been able to take it; she could not break through to life. This then was the defeat she walked with now, the failure of an odyssey that she had hoped might change not only her life but herself.

Defeat after defeat, she thought wearily. She had not felt so depressed in months.

It was almost two o'clock when she came out upon the avenue that followed the harbor to the hotels. There was a slight breeze from the Mediterranean and the sky was an arc of rich blue over the blue harbor. She was very tired and it seemed to her that her life lay about her in pieces, like a tower of blocks that had been leveled. She walked slowly up the boulevard, pausing once to watch from a distance two fishermen folding up their nets. They had kind, friendly brown faces; one of them glanced up and waved at her and Melissa smiled and waved back. The gesture brought contact and she walked on feeling a little less isolated. Those fishermen at least had souls, she thought; they felt life through the touch of simplicities, the fish they caught, the nets they mended, the sound of the sea and the feel of the earth. They did not retreat inside of themselves until a smile was like the breaking of congealed flesh and a wave of the hand like the breaking of wood.

Ahead of her lay a small triangle of park, fashioned out of flowers and grass for the weary. On impulse Melissa walked in among its line of well-pruned hedge and sat down on a bench within the triangle. She realized that she had been wandering for nearly two hours; she had not known how tired she was, and how weary of restless movement. Her feet ached and she felt utterly wretched. She lifted her face to the sun, which held in it the heat of noon, and as the sun warmed her face it mingled on her cheeks with the faint pleasant breeze from the water. Melissa looked out upon the boats, the water, the clipped green hedges and at two old women in black gossiping with their heads together across the path from her.

The act of affixing these things in her mind soothed her for she had gazed without seeing all morning. She sat very still, her hands in her lap, and slowly, softly the tension began to slip away from her, turning this into a good moment, a tranquil moment, after a day of narrowing and anger. And as she let go of her fears, life began to flow into and through her again, melting the walls she had intricately erected to keep herself untouched, unhurt, and unlived. With this hushedness there came over her a strange tenderness, a feeling of presences, so that she felt, almost reverently, that she was not alone, after all, but was a part of this world, of the sky and the air and the sun and the sea and the brilliant flowers, she was a part of life anywhere in this world, homeless yet at home. Here in the sun in Palma, Majorca, she needed no one; it was enough simply to be here, and to be alive.

Surely, she thought, although she was blind to it, life had meaning. She felt this suddenly with absolute certainty. Its meaning was not discernible to her, and perhaps not to any other human being because it must be a very large pattern imposed upon the smaller human pattern, the greater one remaining indecipherable to humans who had not yet learned a larger language. Yet when she looked back upon her life now, upon the darkness of the past that she had endured, the fact that she was sitting here in a park in Majorca seemed miraculous and incredible to her. There had been no discernible signs in that past to prepare her for this moment, no hint that she would one day travel an ocean to view her life from this green bench in the sunshine. Yet at the same time, looking back, she saw that, on a deeper, perceptual level, every day of her life had been building inevitably toward this point of time. It was understanding that awed her now. It was as if in some curious manner each human being lived upon two levels: that while they were occupied with an external life of blind, unconscious action, there was also living within them something well-hidden and eternal, a deeper intelligence which—when it spoke—they must obey or deny at the risk of losing the eternal. It was how each person answered this that ultimately gave or denied meaning to their lives.

She closed her eyes, savoring the warmth of feeling again and of being at peace. Wisdom was like a hand laid across her heart and speaking in a still small voice. It was very sweet. And softly, in this tenderness, she remembered Adam. "Adam," she whispered, and feeling a tug of pain she opened her eyes to meet the curious glances of the two women seated across from her on the opposite bench. At once they glanced away and resumed their gossiping but now Melissa looked at them and really saw them, each in dusty black, their faces round and stolid and roughened by wind and labor. But they were women, too, she thought in astonishment, they as well as herself and the flawless woman in the Paris café who had driven Adam from her; all of them were joined together by the common denominator of humanness.

She looked again into the coarsened features of the two women, imagining their lives, and she thought, "But nothing like Adam ever happened to them, or ever could." If once or twice they had felt great beauty, then it had long since been covered over by the silt of time and dreariness. Why had she allowed cynicism to diminish the only real and lovely experience that had ever happened to her? She thought, "It wasn't external beauty that drew Adam, no matter what his original motive, it was kindredness of spirit. We enjoyed each other." She had forgotten this. Like a hypochondriac she had sought for hurt, she had injected pain into his memory so that she might reject him. Why—because he was never to be possessed, never to be seen again? She had always resisted life because of its pain, but did she not—by demanding too much—use the pain of loss to keep life at a distance? She saw now that this was the greatest cruelty of all, for to turn the heart away from beauty was to murder both beauty and the heart. Out of some arrogant, unmet, neurotic need she had begun subtly to distort and corrupt the first reality she had ever met and trusted. She had reached out to Adam and given: was this not enough? Was not experience enough, if one did not demand its permanence?

She thought in astonishment, "I have always demanded proofs. Proofs that I am loved, that I matter, that I am missed; proofs that I exist, and yes—now I look for some magic signs that it is worthwhile for me to go on living. Today is not enough, I must have proof that tomorrow will be better and easier."

She sighed. "Nor is this all," she realized sadly. "I've always demanded rewards as well, for proofs and rewards go hand in hand. I want—even now—a reward for having come this far alone. I want someone to say, 'Well done, Melissa, you've suffered enough alone, now go home and rest a little.' But there isn't anyone to say this."

Proofs and rewards! This then was why she had begun rejecting Adam—because he had not, after all, been a reward, he had only briefly entered her life and then left forever and now she had no existing proof that she mattered to him.

She thought softly, "But I have learned this much about

reality: life cannot be sustained by proof. Something else has to take its place."

"Faith," she thought in astonishment.

Faith—it was a beautiful word, and one so fraught with risk that she trembled before it. Faith . . . for lacking faith she must forever be condemned to Charles' circle of safety. Faith meant trusting, it meant the horror of trusting the unknown, of placing faith in what could neither be seen nor touched nor proven. It meant going on when one's very soul cried out to turn back, it meant, above all, unending risk.

She thought, "But Adam was a gift, not a reward. How could I have been so blind?" She realized that in this quiet moment she had arrived at the most dangerous crossroad of her life: whether to commit herself wholeheartedly to a life without guarantees, or to continue distrusting life, escaping it, and waiting eternally for the consoling arm of rescue.

"Faith," she thought, trying out the sound of it on her tongue. "I believe . . . I believe," she whispered. "If I believe at this moment in what happened to me in Copenhagen . . . if I believe in the reality that was Adam . . . if I believe in what happened between two people from opposite corners of the world, meeting briefly, never to meet again . . . if I believe that this could happen, and did, then I must believe also that life is worth *trusting* . . ."

She thought suddenly, "I have been given three gifts of value, and perhaps the greatest test of my life is in what I do with them. I have been given the gift of freedom to begin a different, wiser life—if I dare. In Copenhagen I was given an experience of rare beauty which I may reject or use—if I dare.

"And yes—even this—I have been given a package of value, Stearns said so, to deliver safely here. And if I choose to take the first two gifts and carry them farther as responsibilities to myself—why, then I must discharge this third responsibility, too, or all of them will fail."

It was this knowledge then that she had been carrying with her today and resisting. For if life had meaning, and if Adam was a part of its meaning, then Stearns was a part of it, too. For what Stearns had in effect given her was what she had spent her entire life evading: responsibility.

"Of course I don't have to," she thought mechanically. "I don't want to, and Stearns had no right to involve me, no right at all." She had only to forget the book, take it home with her or throw it away and no one would ever know. Stearns had died for this package after all.

Yet if she chose to commit herself unquestioningly to life—?

She stood up and began walking, very quickly now, because she was not just a woman traveling alone or a meaningless statistic, she had substance and content, she was herself, Melissa Aubrey, and she was going to have to deliver Stearns' book for him. She had known for a long time that she must, but around this knowledge she had built higher and higher walls until she had erected a maze in which she herself had become lost. Now she must carry out this bequest of a dead man, just as she'd had to leave the ship at Bremerhaven and compel herself toward Copenhagen, and then to Paris and at last Majorca, not willingly—and always unready—but growing to each new change. And perhaps this was all there was to life, the growing and the anguish of it, the going on and the trusting to new possibilities. How was she to know if she hung back? How was she to know unless she tried?

"My key please, 297," she told the desk clerk.

"Sí, Señora," he said, smiling at her radiance.

She took the key and hurried to her room to find Stearns' book.

# 15

THERE WERE TWO MEN IN BLACK WAITING IN THE LOBBY when she stepped from the elevator; she saw them standing near the door of the souvenir shop glancing over postcards. She did not underestimate the care she must exercise in losing them or the cleverness needed to outwit them. She had first understood this when she confronted Stearns' book in her room, recognizing its significance in their eyes and feeling suddenly very self-conscious about separating it from her other books. When she had slipped it into the right-hand pocket of her trench coat, she had added a second paperback book to her left pocket, and then she had picked up a third to carry in her hand on the supposition that the presence of three books would conceal or confuse the significance of the one.

Pausing now in the center of the lobby she conspicuously brought out her map of Palma to examine. Reestablishing the location of the Veri Rosario she looked for a central point and found it in the street that contained in one short row the telephone company, the police station, and the post office. Very good, she thought, she would take a taxi to the Gran Via José Antonio and dismiss it at the post office, an act which should obscure her real destination to the two men if they eavesdropped, and—hopefully—divert them when they followed her. Moving very suddenly she walked outside and waved a hand; at once a taxi disengaged itself from the line of waiting cabs. "The Gran Via José Antonio," she said, climbing inside.

"Sí," replied the driver, and pulled just as quickly away from the hotel. Turning, Melissa looked back at a street empty of moving cars, nor did any cars swing precipitately out from the curb as her taxi turned into the traffic of the boulevard to head for the center of town. She continued her rear-window vigil, but her hasty departure did not appear to have been noticed. Certainly it had not caused any obvious flurry of activity behind her: it was nearing siesta time and the boulevard was nearly devoid of traffic, the only car in sight was pulling up now beside the harbor to deliver three children and a woman to the pavement. A feeling of infinite relief filled Melissa; she had not expected to lose them so quickly. This time, by moving swiftly and engaging a taxi instead of walking, she had succeeded in surprising them. And high time, she thought, for she had submitted long enough to their shadowing, until the weight of their presence had diminished and dispirited her.

They were approaching the government buildings on the Gran Via José Antonio. Impulsively she leaned forward and spoke into the driver's ear. "The Plaza Veri Rosario, please."

"Sí—what number?"

"I will tell you when we get there."

He nodded, and swerved to avoid a dog crossing the street. Her heart was beating rapidly now as she leaned forward to watch the street signs. When she spied the words Plaza Veri Rosario her throat went dry for this was a name she had lived with for a very long time, and then the taxi turned and entered the charming street that she had unwittingly visited on the preceding day. Ahead she saw the protruding sign of the Anglo-Majorcan Export Company. "Number eleven, please," she said, and opening her purse she began fumbling for pesetas.

The tires of the cab scraped the curb as it slowed to a stop. Pesetas in hand Melissa had one hand on the knob of the door when it was abruptly wrenched open from the outside. A man insinuated his body through the door and fell into the seat beside her. Melissa said indignantly, "Look here—" and then she gasped as the taxi abruptly pulled out from the curb and sped at breakneck speed past Anglo-Majorcan Exports.

"How dare you," cried Melissa, and leaning forward she pounded on the driver's back. "Stop! I haven't gotten out yet! Stop this car immediately!"

But the driver ignored her, and the man beside her pulled her back against the seat. It had never occurred to her that the taxi driver might be one of them, it was like a nightmare, they had people everywhere like spiders weaving a web around her: the taxi driver, the two men at the hotel, and a man outside the Anglo-Majorcan Export Company, each of them watching for this single moment of weakness—or strength—on her part.

"Stop," she said again, but feebly.

"The car will not stop," said the man seated next to her, and to add punctuation to his statement he drew a pistol from his pocket and laid it across his lap, one finger caressing the trigger.

"Look here," she said, trying again, "I'm an American and you can't do this. If it's money you want, I'll give you what I have. Just take it and let me out."

The man beside her yawned boredly.

"It amounts to kidnaping, you know," she said angrily, "and there are laws against kidnaping." But she was speaking into a void. Damn these voids, she thought peevishly, and subsided. She thought of offering to sign over all her travelers' checks as a bribe, she thought of attempting to jump from the car but a sense of great futility swept over her, for it was not money they were after, and what was the point of deluding herself? It was Stearns' book they wanted. Stearns—always Stearns, she thought furiously.

Tears came to her eyes, and because she was beginning to feel very frightened she straightened her shoulders and sat up, hands crossed in her lap, as if posture alone might conceal from these men the frailness of the woman they were abducting. They must not know she was afraid.

The cab had left the central part of the town and was threading its way through streets lined with shuttered, pastel-colored pensions and villas. Siesta time had arrived and the streets had emptied themselves of people. Their progress felt increasingly unreal to Melissa. With each passing street she felt smaller and more fragile, her sense of identity was being stripped from her and left behind on the road like so many scraps of paper that the wind would soon scatter—and then who would Melissa Aubrey be? That was the horror of it. "Only nothing," she thought, her throat tightening with grief. *The wind passeth over it and it is gone; and the place thereof shall know it no more.*

The cab slowed and turned and Melissa glanced up to see a wall of hibiscus and a wrought-iron gate. Ahead lay a sandy crescent-shaped drive leading up to a white stucco villa almost concealed by espaliered trees and vines. They were still in Palma and they had reached their destination. The car drew up to a secluded front door decorated with lacy grillwork behind which stood glass, framed in cedar. Melissa closed her eyes and braced herself, thinking, "Like Stearns you may have to die for this, Melissa."

She had named it now: death.

She was frightened but as they opened the door of the car she could feel her weakness tighten into a magnificent strength-giving fear. She saw that what she had experienced before was anxiety, which was formless and had devoured her without focus, but behind these walls lay the source of her terror, someone human and knowable whom she must face at last. And realizing this she felt her anxieties knit themselves into this defiant, angry, splendid fear, and it was beautiful to feel again. Fear was strengthening, fear brought challenge and a racing of the pulse, fear galvanized and healed and drew together; her fear was a thing of beauty, making her alive again and real and very human, and out of it was born the same heightened awareness, the same exalted sense of life that she had felt with Adam, so that she became capable—in the moment between car and house—of seeing light and shadow, green and scarlet, death and life, as she had neither seen nor felt them before.

Walking between the two men she passed through the wrought-iron door and into a long, polished hall.

She was taken into a room at the end of the long hall, and presently a small woman in a dusty black dress came in and with gestures indicated that Melissa was to be searched. Her wristwatch, purse, and coat were given immediately to someone outside, and then Melissa was forced to disrobe and submit to a thorough search of her clothes and her body. It was humiliating and it was insulting, and only Melissa's anger carried her through it.

When the woman was finished Melissa was allowed to dress again, and both her purse and her coat were returned to her. Surprisingly, the two paperback books remained in its pockets.

"Vamos. De se usted prisa," the woman said harshly, and without understanding the words Melissa guessed that she was to follow her. They walked down a hall whose shining floor reflected in its surface the flowers on a mahogany stand and the lacy grillwork of the door at the other end. This time they entered a large library, and Melissa was told to sit. The woman left, and almost at once a man entered the room from a small corner door.

He surprised Melissa. He wore a strikingly iridescent gray suit—Adam would have approved, she thought wryly —with trousers tapering to a dramatic leanness. His white shirt was ruffled, and he wore a scarlet string tie. His face was dark, wise and clever. There was a faint suggestion of a mustache no heavier than a pencil line—this was a man who overdid nothing. He said to her with a flash of white teeth, "But you are very attractive." He drew out a damask-covered chair behind the small rosewood desk and gestured her to a matching chair behind it. "Do join me," he begged.

She had not expected anyone so charming, so suave, and she braced herself as she walked to the chair he indicated. She sat down, and he seated himself across the desk and regarded her with interest. "Permit me to introduce myself," he said. "I am Señor Castigar."

"I am Mrs. Aubrey," she told him warily.

"Yes, of course. We have been following you for quite some time." He was watching her closely, awaiting her reaction to this.

She said evenly, "You have kidnapped me and submitted me to a search and I should like to remind you that I am an American citizen."

He smiled faintly. "But we are not going to take your American citizenship from you. All that we want from you is the Baikonur code which the man Stearns gave to you. And we want it now."

"Baikonur code," she repeated.

"Sí."

"I have never heard of a Baikonur code," she told him.

He gestured this aside impatiently. "It scarcely matters since you are not—I don't think—an agent. We wish what Stearns gave to you, and what you were about to deliver to number eleven, Plaza Veri Rosario."

"But you've searched me," she pointed out. "You didn't find any code, did you?"

"We scarcely expected to," returned the Señor. "Of course one always hopes—" He shrugged. "But Stearns was a man on the run; there was not the time for him either to notify Washington of his fantastic discovery—a factor in our favor—or, alas, to put it into a suitable form for traveling. But once he knew he was to die he gave you *something*. And what he gave to you, whether tangible or memorizable, he put into a form understandable to the Anglo-Majorcan Export Company. Presently you will tell us what he gave to you, please."

She said indignantly, "What makes you so sure of that?"

He shrugged. "If you do not tell us then you will die."

She said quickly, "If you kill me then you will never learn what Stearns gave me!"

His smile was silky. "I do not think you understand the situation, Mrs. Aubrey. The Baikonur code is ours, it belongs to us. What is of supreme importance is to prevent your people from acquiring the Baikonur code. It would quite frankly be a catastrophe to us, exposing the nature of certain secret documents which your people already possess but which they cannot decipher. They would learn at once, for instance, of one particular alliance in the Mediterranean that would change the entire nature of the Conference which begins tomorrow morning."

She laughed. "But if this is your code what is the point of your needing to hear from me what you already know? Why not simply kill me?"

He smiled faintly. "You see that. However, if you see this then perhaps you can understand also that possessing the essential key to any code is like the unraveling of wool, it can work in either direction, for us as well as for your people. For your experts to decipher the Baikonur code Stearns would have had to specify a clue—a key—that would unlock the Baikonur code by means of one of your American codes. The opposite is also true. If we learn with what key your experts were to unscramble our Baikonur code—which we already know—then by working in reverse our experts may have some hope of deciphering *your* code."

"Oh," she said, and into her mind leaped the words *George is very sick.* Was this the key? she wondered.

"This is why you have some importance," went on Señor Castigar. "Some usefulness to us alive, and why I am instructed to deal with you as a person of some use to us. But do not underestimate your situation, you remain entirely helpless. It is not known in Washington or in Majorca that Stearns had the fantastic luck to steal the Baikonur code from us. Your Central Intelligence is aware that he was murdered, but at the moment they are completely in the dark as to why, and why he was traveling by ship under a false identity."

She said coolly, "I think you underestimate them, Señor. They know very well that Stearns was carrying something of infinite value to the Conference here."

Señor Castigar said lightly, "Oh? And how do you know this?"

"I was visited in Paris by a CIA agent."

Señor Castigar smiled. "On the contrary the CIA entered the picture only three days ago when they sent an agent here to Palma to question you, a gentleman by the name of Mr. Marc West."

"Marc West?" She stared at him in horror. "I don't believe you," she gasped.

He smiled. "You must not think all CIA agents are as intelligent as Stearns."

"I still don't believe you," she said flatly.

"No?" He lifted one eyebrow. "That is because you are perhaps remembering Grimes, but he was one of our men." Señor Castigar leaned back comfortably in his chair. "Come now, Mrs. Aubrey, you must see that you are very ill-equipped to cope with international espionage. It is quite useless to fight me, you have no weapons."

"Grimes," she echoed, appalled. "But—then nothing he told me was true?"

"On the contrary everything that he told you was true. We remained certain that you must be the person we looked for, but it became a strong possibility that you had forgotten Stearns, or had dismissed him as a hysteric. It became vital that you know precisely who Stearns was. A little pressure, a little enlightenment, a small appeal to your patriotism appeared in order."

She said dryly, "You are indeed very clever." She hesitated, and then, rigidly controlling her voice added, "There was another man—in Copenhagen. Was he, Adam Burrill, one of your men also?"

Señor Castigar shrugged. "I could of course say yes, but actually he was a total stranger to us. Now I have been extremely frank with you, you will please be equally as frank with me."

But Melissa was rallying. "I think not," she said coolly.

"You prefer death then," he said harshly.

"But I am not afraid to die," she said, and was surprised

to realize that at this moment it was almost true, and that she did not speak out of bravado. What Stearns had given her possessed value—which gave meaning even to death —and she had just learned that her trust in Adam, so timidly, hopefully given, had not been misplaced.

Señor Castigar was regarding her with amusement. "Now that is very interesting—and quite improbable." With scorn he said, "Everybody is afraid to die, I do not believe you."

She smiled. "Nevertheless, for the first time in my life —I feel this—it won't matter as it used to."

He said dryly, "You must by all means tell me your secret formula."

She said steadily, with a lift of her head, "In the past weeks I have experienced enough—just enough, you understand—to feel what it can be like to be really alive."

He shrugged. "All the better to continue life then!"

At this moment, holding her future lightly, he seemed to her very earth-bound and obtuse. She shook her head, feeling her way toward the truth of this. "Perhaps we clutch at life only when we have never lived or trusted it. Then death seems the last and greatest defeat, the end of something never felt." She lifted her head and looked at him. "Now I have experienced just enough to make it"—she shrugged—"possible. Not welcome, you understand, but —if necessary—bearable."

"I see," he said, studying her face. "And so death does not frighten you." His eyes suddenly narrowed and he said, "Perhaps life frightens you more."

She gazed at him. "I don't think I know what you mean."

He smiled. "We know something of you, we are very thorough. Your life has seemed difficult lately, no? But you have experienced something on your travels. Yes, I can see that death could feel for you like the good ending, the closing of a symphony on a high note." He leaned back in his chair and his smile was amused. "So you are ready then to meet death, even torture, with great nobility?"

"Or as best I can," she said.

"Very good." His smile deepened. "Then I will not condemn you to death, my dear, nor even to torture. I shall condemn you instead to the more exquisite torture: to living."

She stared at him in astonishment.

"And the emptiest living possible." He leaned forward and his lip curled. "You have had a glorious experience? It will pass. I will let Time work its way on you, my dear, for I am in no hurry as yet. You are neither saint nor mystic, I will banish you to isolation—to solitary confinement—where day by day, hour by hour, minute by minute, you will experience—why, nothing at all. For nothing lasts—above all these brief, daring flights into life. You will learn soon enough that there is no meaning in life, that all of life is meaningless." He rang a bell. "Arturo," he told the man who appeared, "take her downstairs to the cell and lock her inside."

Melissa felt a whisper of uneasiness. She stood and looked curiously at Señor Castigar, and he looked at her with a little smile playing about his lips.

"You see?" he said. "Even your courage was meaningless."

She wordlessly followed Arturo out of the room.

# 16

Arturo left, closing and locking the iron door behind him, and there remained only the deep, implacable silence of an uninhabited place. Melissa stood with her coat over one arm. She could feel the door at her back; if she took but one step forward she would stumble across the bare sheet of plywood that had been laid across metal juts to make a cot. High above her—far beyond reach—hung a small square window from which light came. This was her cell, no longer than six feet, no wider than five, the dimensions of a cement tomb.

She sat down suddenly on the bunk and placed her coat across her lap. It made a small rustling sound that shocked the silence. She noted that there was no window in the door—she was to be spared the horror of being watched, at least—and they had left her both coat and purse, but this was no consolation either. She could not believe just now that this had happened to her. A part of her stood off at a great distance so that she was divided and unfeeling. She felt a little cold, that was all, as one does when frozen. Yet she did not shiver; this chill was deep inside. She thought coldly, "Something is happening to me," but she did not feel it. She couldn't understand, couldn't grasp the why of this when she had behaved so well. Everything had gone terribly wrong. Hadn't God heard her when she had sat in the park and pledged herself to life, hadn't she made it clear to God that she was doing this, not just for herself, but also for Stearns? She had been resigned even to dying for Stearns' book, and this gesture, so implicitly selfless, had been wasted and even laughed at. Had her vows fallen on deaf ears?

"It should have been different," she whispered. "It shouldn't have happened this way; I don't understand." She had cast off her fears and acted, and for this first positive act of her life there should have been an answering affirmation, even applause and praise, but instead she was being punished, for how else could she construe being hurled into a cell? Punishment . . . it was ironic when there should instead have been a handwrought miracle waiting for her. A happy ending. *An Adam.*

Oh, if only it could have happened the way she'd assumed it would: she saw herself shaking off her pursuers to walk at last into the Anglo-Majorcan Export Company. She saw the shop as long, narrow, and dim, its counters piled high with colorful fabrics. The man in the rear of the shop looked pleasant, paternal, and very British. She saw herself walk up to him to say coolly, "I have here a small package given me by a mutual friend of ours named Stearns." She pictured his growing astonishment, the open mouth and incredulous eyes. "You knew Stearns? You know then *why* he was murdered?"

"Yes." Again coolly, "He was bringing you the Baikonur code."

"The Baikonur code!" he gasped. "Good God! Fantastic!"

"It's why he was murdered, of course." She would slip the book across the counter. "I was also to tell you that page 191 is of vital importance, and give you the message that George is very sick."

"George is very sick."

"Yes."

He would shake his head incredulously. "But if he was murdered for this how on earth did you manage to get through? I know the people who murdered him—ruthless and shrewd, all of them. And the Baikonur code—how can we ever repay you! But come, you are exhausted, I see this. Come into the back office for a little tea and tell us everything. How on earth you ever managed to get here when we're constantly watched—but what courage, I am speechless. You're not traveling alone, are you?"

"Quite alone."

"Good God!"

He would press a buzzer, or speak into a telephone, and at once his assistant would appear, a tall and distinguished young man named Cartwright who subtly resembled Adam. "He too is in The Game, my dear, you may speak openly. Cartwright, lock the front door, will you? Hang up a sign, we're taking our siesta early today."

Admiration. Consolation. The childish fantasy faded. Proofs and rewards, thought Melissa wearily—but how did one function without them? What else was there? The kind word, the soothing hand on the brow—She pressed trembling hands to her temples. Longingly she recalled her past innocence and longingly yearned for its return, for if this was reality—this raw and brutal end to an effort of promise—then it had obviously been an act of genius on her part to avoid both life and reality. One could bruise oneself over and over again, it seemed, and still find no meaning, no reason for which to go on. This very cell was proof of this: she would die here and no one would ever know, nor would there be anyone to mourn her at this half-way point between two lives: her parents were dead, Charles was already a part of the past, and to Dr. Szym she was only a patient. And Adam—tears of self-pity dimmed her eyes as she realized that Adam would never know. He would mail his Christmas note, and when he received none from her he would reflect sadly upon her shallowness and the brevity of her memory.

If she could only cry she might feel again, she thought, but she was too numb to cry. "Perhaps tomorrow I can cry," she thought. Tomorrow? But she could not believe that tomorrow she would still be here, she could not believe that life could be so brutal. Surely at any moment Señor Castigar would open the cell door and say, "It has been a little joke to test you, Señora, but now you may come out . . ."

"I am in a cell," she said aloud, again trying to make it feel real to her. A part of her responded, saying, "But what on earth are you doing in a cell?" and she nodded mutely. "Yes, isn't it preposterous? That's why it's so unreal. It can't be true, I won't let it be true." She reached out a hand and touched the wall, which was not smooth after all, but pebbly because it was made of stucco. She drew her hand very quickly down the wall and this hurt, and she had a faint sensation of having briefly established a relationship between herself and the wall because when the contact hurt she knew the wall was there. "A promising sado-masochistic relationship," she thought dryly, and quickly dropped her hand. She wished they had not taken her wristwatch from her because she was sure that all this would be easier for her if she knew the time. She brought out the mystery novel that she had carried with her and settled down to read it but the words proved meaningless for between her eyes and the page stood an invisible barrier of anxiety so that her mind remained rigid and stunned and she had to read whole paragraphs a second time and then a third time yet was still unable to grasp their meaning. She forced her eyes to continue following the lines even as her dialogue continued . . . "I want to go home, this is not the way life should be, I cannot believe this is happening, I refuse to believe it . . ."

She thought suddenly—and it briefly pierced the fog—"A part of me does know this is real." Was it that she had long ago made up her own reality, like a child fashioning a make-believe world, and then forever after selected only what fitted into a pre-conceived pattern? She thought, "It isn't that I cannot find reality, it's I who evade it when I glimpse it, I drive it from me with incredible contortions of mind."

Several hours later a tray was thrust inside her cell, the door immediately closing again. Melissa glanced with apathy at the food, then arose and wearily lifted the tray to her lap. Señor Castigar ate well: the food was strange to her but palatable and nourishing. When she had finished eating the light in her cell had grown dimmer, and she realized that soon it would be dark.

Dark . . . it seemed just now the greatest horror of all. She was alone, and night was coming. Was it truly only illusion that she was alone, as Dr. Szym had implied? But if one had no real sense of God, or even of belonging to life, then it became necessary to draw support from people, and there were no people here and there would be none. She was thousands of miles from home, completely cut off from friends and familiar surroundings by both distance and time, and what was worse, she was locked away in a cell in the home of a Majorcan madman. She tried to conceive of some realistic manner in which her disappearance could have been noted: in novels there would have been someone passing the Anglo-Majorcan Export Company at the moment of her abduction who would have immediately understood the abruptness of the taxi's departure and witnessed the look of horror on her face, and drawing the proper conclusions would have written down the cab's number and gone off at once to the police.

But there weren't going to be any witnesses, there never were, not in real life. And even if someone had seen the incident—which was visually impossible—who on earth would take even a moment to speculate on foul play or to become involved in such a matter?

There was the hotel, of course . . . There at least she was a paying guest, with a room number, a name, and luggage still in her room. Yes, they might wonder about a missing guest—but not until another day had passed, and then the maid would only conclude with a smile that the señora was due to check out, and then they would ring to ask if she planned to stay longer. But meeting no success how long would it be before they deduced that something had happened to the American señora? Days perhaps. Hotels did not welcome mysteries and perhaps, like herself, they avoided facing facts as long as possible.

What then?

"Not a single clue," she whispered. "Not one single blasted hint of where I might have gone, or what could have happened to me." Her passport was in the hotel safe. In her suitcase the police might find the copy of her passport photograph and with this they could approach the cab drivers and bellhops at the front door, but by that time the trail would be very cold. The police would have to deduce that she had not left the island legally but that she might have left it illegally. Eventually, in time, they would learn from the Carmichael Travel Agency in Bruxton, Massachusetts, that Melissa Aubrey was a very legal person, and this would distress them because then they would have to assume that something very wicked had happened to her on their lovely island. But still they would have no way of guessing in what she could have become involved. The one man in Palma to whom she could have run for help was the same man from whom she had fled in terror. . . .

For that matter, knowing about Marc West, it was quite possible that Señor Castigar had smoothly explained her absence to the hotel in advance, and that she was no longer even a guest there.

In any case she was utterly without hope of rescue. She had almost literally been wiped off the face of the earth. She was here, and no one would ever know that she was here, and at the full realization of her helplessness she felt panic well up inside her and knew she was going to scream in a moment. She did scream and, frightened, waited for footsteps or a reply. There were neither, there was only this unending silence, as if the world outside had ceased to be and she was the only person alive. Her worst nightmare had come true: the world had abandoned her. "Dear God, how can you do this to me," she cried. "What have I done to deserve this?" She began to cry with enormous engulfing

sobs until—most terrifying of all—there came to her the
words that Charles had used over and over when she left
him: "How can you do this to me," he had cried. "What
have I done to deserve this?"

The cell door opened, letting in light. Had it been a
dream then, had rescue come after all, was it really a joke?
Arturo stood framed in the doorway holding a flashlight.
"You will come," he said. "The Señor will see you before
he retires for the night."

No, it had not been a dream. Wordlessly Melissa followed him through the dark labyrinth of a cellar, up
wooden stairs and into a brilliantly lit kitchen. The lights
staggered her: lights beating down on glittering white tile
walls, light playing across white porcelain freezers, lights
striking glints across aluminum-doored cupboards, and
light captured by great copper pots suspended from the
ceiling. Melissa was blinded and put a hand over her eyes.

"This way," bid Arturo.

This was a home, and she was homeless. People lived
here—and she was brought up from a dark cell in the earth
where there was not even a mattress for her bed. Beware,
she thought, feeling familiar waves of grief sweep through
her.

Señor Castigar was waiting for her in the same room.
Flowers at his desk. Long silken curtains drawn across the
windows. The sheen of mahogany. It was a beautiful room
and its delicacies were an assault to the senses after the
bleakness of her cell. On the mantel she saw a marble
clock: it was three o'clock in the morning.

"Ah yes, Mrs. Aubrey," said Señor Castigar in his damnably kind, suave voice. But he did not suggest a chair this
time nor rise at her entrance, and her nerves trembled at
this rebuff. He remained comfortably seated, examining
his fingernails with interest. "I have dined out," he said,
and glanced up, but although his glance was swift and brief
she was aware that it was clinically thorough and missed
neither the tear-stained cheeks nor the sullen eyes. "Before
retiring I thought—because I like you—"

Damn him, she thought, feeling her heart lift at these words.

"—that I would ask if you see the folly of your ways after twelve hours of reflection in my little cell. There is, you see, no need for you to remain down there. You have only to discuss Stearns with me and you will become a guest in my house."

She nodded. A guest in his house.

"You see, I will not bring you up here again," he pointed out softly. "I wish you to understand this. You will not see this room again."

She nodded.

"Now supposing you sit down and tell me what Stearns gave to you."

"No," she said.

He shrugged. "But you see there is no point to your suffering like this when you can spend the rest of the night in my guest room and be returned to your hotel in the morning."

He was offering her life again, he was offering her the hotel and a return to the new life she had only begun. Longing stirred in her and at this moment it occurred to her that to choose death over life must be the most unrealistic act of all.

"Perhaps you do not believe me when I say I will let you leave," he told her softly. "But you see, I can be fairly sure that you would avoid the Anglo-Majorcan Export Company. It is not a pleasant experience, becoming a traitor to one's own country, but you would have the pleasant compensation of being a live traitor. Now. Of what possible use is this attitude of yours?"

She bit her lip. "I don't know."

He smiled charmingly. "It is so very meaningless. You are here, there is no hope, you will remain here and in time you will die." Ever so subtly his voice stressed the latter phrase. "What are you proving? There is no one to prove anything to. Stearns? He is dead. Me? Well, really, what difference do I make? I only take orders. The Anglo-Majorcan Export Company? They do not even know of your existence, and never will."

He was so damnably right. "I don't know," she said numbly, and she didn't know.

"Give up, my dear," he said, watching her closely. "What is the use of this nonsense?"

"I don't know," she repeated dully.

He sat back. "You have so many years ahead. Love, marriage—" He hesitated and then drew from his pocket an envelope which he placed on his desk. "This was intercepted at your hotel this afternoon."

She stared at unfamiliar writing addressed to herself at her hotel in Mallorca, Español. She said, "That is no one I know."

"It is signed Adam." He was watching her with narrowed eyes.

Adam? She regarded Señor Castigar with some astonishment, and then she remembered that she had asked him earlier about Adam, naming him, and she understood that this was another trick to persuade her back to life. "You are very clever, Señor," she said wearily.

"I see that you are not familiar with the handwriting," he said forgivingly. "But you have in your wallet a slip of paper—an address—with writing that matches this. I compared them."

She said with tired scorn, "You forged the writing, then, of course."

"You are stubborn," said Señor Castigar with a sigh. He drew a single sheet of paper from the envelope and placed it on the desk between them. "You may read the last few lines," he said. "They are personal enough, perhaps, to reassure you of what you cannot seem to believe. Later when you cooperate you may have the whole letter."

She leaned over the desk, perversely glancing first at the phrases at the top of the letter which Señor Castigar's fingers did not entirely conceal. Her eye caught fragments here and there:

    . . . awoke in the middle of the night . . . that hypothetical situation which I so heedlessly dismissed . . . and then recalling . . . in his atrocious hot tweeds and . . .

"Adam?" she thought tremulously, something stirring in her deeply.

Señor Castigar's hand moved to cover what she had been reading, and now her glance dropped to the last lines.

*I must hear from you at once that you are all right,* Adam wrote. *When you receive this I will be reaching Zurich, the Hotel Trümpy. Telephone me collect. My darling, am I to forever remember and worry about you?*

"Oh Adam," she thought sadly, knowing that nothing could be changed now, that it was too late, that she was here and yet might not be here if Adam's letter had reached her earlier, diverting her from what she had to do. She thought, "It must not matter too much, I must not think about this or Señor Castigar will use it as a tool to get what he wishes. Nothing has changed, or can. It has to be enough just to know that he wrote these lines, that he did not too quickly forget."

"Well?"

She mutely shook her head.

His lips thinned. He said curtly, "Very well then, I can have no more patience with you. I have discovered since I last saw you that I must leave Palma tomorrow afternoon, and since I certainly have no intention of leaving you here alive I think you can draw your own conclusions. You understand?"

To be shocked was a relative thing: she had already sustained several shocks and now a faraway part of her was both amused and surprised to realize that she could be shocked again—she felt it in the icy shiver that went down her spine—in the awareness that even this small circle of safety was about to shrink. She could not cling to anything. There was nothing left.

Señor Castigar said crisply, "I will give you until one o'clock tomorrow afternoon—no, *this* afternoon, for the day has begun—to decide whether you wish to live or die.

At that hour Arturo serves lunch. He will arrive with your tray and you may tell him your decision."

She carefully wet her lips. "And how—that is, what means do you use for killing your prisoners?" As soon as she had spoken she was sorry to have betrayed her weakness.

He smiled, obviously pleased that she had asked. "Oh, I am quite humane," he said, "and very up-to-date. Your cell is actually a gas chamber, equipped with two pipes for the entry of gas. Two people have already died there."

She nodded dumbly. Two people had already died there. But horror piled upon horror only brought a different feeling of unrealness to her, and death was death after all, no matter how it arrived.

"Unless," he said carefully, not looking at her, "you care to talk about this now."

She longed to say Yes, longed to deliver herself of this weight of fear and conflict, and for a moment she wavered yet knew that somehow—for what reason she didn't know —she must hang on if only because, without realness, she must stubbornly make it as difficult as possible both for herself and for this man to get what each wanted: for him the book, for herself freedom.

He opened the drawer of his desk and brought out a wristwatch and she recognized it as hers. "You may take this back with you," he said pointedly. "You may watch each of the hours fly past and reflect upon a life that has much promise, if you only learn the art of compromise. I give you until one o'clock today. Good-by," he said in an indifferent voice, and his contempt was another wound.

Arturo led her back into the depths of the house and to the cell that was now as black and silent as a tomb, and this time when the door closed behind her it rang with a new finality. It appeared that having committed herself to life only a number of hours ago she had sentenced herself to death.

She began to shiver inconsolably.

# 17

Sometime during the course of the long black night—propped up against the wall, her coat around her shoulders—some semblance of understanding began to stir in Melissa, as if deep inside of her a long battle had raged and been lost, and now—but only now—she could acknowledge her defeat and begin slowly, humbly to count her dead and dying illusions. She began first of all with an acceptance of where she was, and an acceptance of the fact that she had committed herself to helping Stearns—it no longer mattered why—and that she had failed. And having failed, she must therefore pay the price and pay it alone: this much was irrevocable. And perhaps, she thought, it was only justice that she make the acquaintance of failure now, for in avoiding failure all of her life she had also avoided success. She was a stranger to both.

Yet it was strange to count over her losses and routs and discover one missing: it had not occurred to her—not seriously at least—to give Señor Castigar the book that he wanted, and this was a piece that did not fit the puzzle of herself. She examined this with a curious detachment and asked herself if she could buy back her new life with Stearns' book. Could she? She wanted very much to live. . . .

She sighed, trying to imagine the Melissa who could rise phoenixlike from the ashes to walk free from this house into the sunshine. She tried to feel that woman, to *be* that woman for a moment; but it was not difficult at all, for she had been that Melissa for all of her life as she ran from risk and responsibility. She saw that to give Señor Castigar the book and walk free from this cell was to remain forever in captivity, and that it was here in this cell that she was truly free, because for the first time in her life she was taking a stand, she was carrying out a commitment that she had made and resisting the delicious ease of purchasing safety for herself at the cost of integrity. For she knew the accompanying despairs of self-betrayal by rote now: the feelings of emptiness and loss, the restless dreams at night, the small escapes that in time interred the spirit. She had already borne their weights, she was an old friend of ease, concealment, and guilt. She had been there before.

Only something better could erase the lost years.

Only a new country—only the terrain of struggle—held any hope for her because it was a route she had never traveled.

Only something better . . .

Was death better?

There were a variety of deaths for a human, she realized with new clarity, and of them all the most horrible was to become no more than an empty but still living shell. Merely to survive was no longer enough. The greatest suffering in life was to live without suffering, to function without soul or integrity, an uninhabited human without feeling, without pain, without hope. If she failed to discharge this first responsibility of her life, given to her by a dead man, the whole structure of her future would be founded upon betrayal.

No, she could not give up Stearns' book.

Melissa dozed, and waking cold and tired she remembered Adam, for Adam was the first realness she had known and she must cling to him now as to a spar. From the window high in the wall near the ceiling came a shaft of light so pale and silvery she thought it might be moonlight. That was real, and the cell was real; and from these two tangibles she must draw conclusions about the intangible, which was Adam. Once—only ten days ago—he had been as touchable as the wall beside her, and then he had vanished into time and space, leaving no proof at all that he had ever existed or was real.

No proof at all, she thought—except in the tenderness he had left behind like a trail of phosphorous.

She sat up and leaned against the wall, her eyes fastened upon the square of moonsilver. It was suddenly urgent to discover what was real. The question was whether *she* existed here alone in this cell, for if *she* was real then Adam was also real. It was this doubt of her own realness that had prevented her from feeling life during those years with Charles, and it was why Charles had made no more impression upon her soul than the silken touch of a feather drawn lightly over a surface. Looking back she thought of herself as having been enclosed in a skin of transparent, hard shell that by the nature of its surface kept all truly felt experience from entering her. She had lived but felt nothing, which was the ultimate isolation. That shell, she remembered, feeling it now in retrospect, had been composed actually of interlocked muscles so tense with anxiety that everything happening to her had been quite literally like water rolling off a duck's back, incapable of penetrating or leaving any imprint or memory.

In her healing this shell had begun to dissolve, she was becoming flesh again, she was beginning—falteringly and spasmodically—to feel once more, to acquire memory, and to people the impoverished country of her mind.

But if people never *experienced* life, she thought with astonishment, then they were forever doomed to emptiness, to loss of touch, to speaking at but never with each other. How many words had never been listened to, she wondered; how many emotions unfelt until life became no more than a play on a stage watched from the alienation of great distance. With Adam she had felt both herself and life and then she had suffered a relapse, doubting both herself and life, because there was no one to explain to her the truth of Adam. But who was he really, she mused, except a man experienced through her own humanness, her reactions screened and sifted through her own responses. To an observer he might have appeared any number of people: a rake, a kindly, disillusioned man, an indulgent playboy, or a ruthless egoist. She had longed for someone to tell her who he was but did it matter who he was when she had been moved with all her senses by *what* he was? Was any response authentic other than her own?

It had been an encounter that had changed her, and this was sufficient measure. It had been neither more nor less than this. It had held for her the perfection of flawless timing and ripeness but another year, even another month, and she might have given and found less. For she forgot that she had contributed something, too. In her desperate search for realness she had demanded an absence of masks between them and perhaps this had changed Adam as well. She would never know. She had met and experienced him alone—and was still alone, as human beings must always be alone—unless they learned to contain experience, she thought, unless they allowed it to penetrate and enter like a presence into the country of their heart. . . .

Then Stearns, too, had been real, she thought, and even in death could remain real to her if she could uncover and remember the essence of him. Recalling the slim pocket flashlight in her purse she brought it out and trained it on the book that was all that she had of him. She had forgotten how worn and used the volume was; it was a book that he must have chosen to carry with him as a private treasure. Holding it up she discovered that the pages opened by themselves to a certain section in the book. She held it up a second time, and again the book opened by itself to the same page and she saw that it contained the concluding paragraph of Emerson's essay on *Compensation*. She read,

*"And yet the compensations of calamity are made ap-*

*parent to the understanding, also, after long intervals of
time . . . The death of a dear friend, wife, brother, lover,
which seemed nothing but privation, somewhat later as-
sumes the aspect of a guide or genius; for it commonly
operates revolutions in our way of life, terminates an
epoch of infancy or of youth waiting to be closed, breaks
up a wonted occupation, or a household, or style of living
. . . and the man or woman who would have remained a
sunny garden flower, with no room for its roots and too
much sunshine for its head, by the falling of the walls and
the neglect of the gardener is made the banyan of the for-
est, yielding shade and fruit to wide neighborhoods of
men . . ."*

She gently closed the book . . . *By the falling of the walls
and the neglect of the gardener* . . . She began to consider
Stearns in relation to these words he must have read over
and over, she began to wonder what lives he had lived
before he became an agent, what calamities he must have
suffered, what hells he might have endured before he met
the final revolution in his life. It took something to mold a
Stearns, she thought, and to her surprise she felt a peculiar
closeness to him now, as if she shared with him something
more than impending death.

"If I met him now," she thought in astonishment, "I
would see him—this time—as a human being."

# 18

THE BANG OF THE BREAKFAST TRAY ON THE FLOOR AWOKE
Melissa, and she opened her eyes, believing she would find
herself at home. She had fallen asleep sitting up and she
was so stiff that it pained her to move. Her concrete dun-
geon was cold this morning and Melissa's head ached, but
what stunned her was to discover that she was still in her
cell, that not even dreams had removed her from it or ex-
orcised the evil spell. She glanced quickly at her wristwatch and realized it was eight o'clock in the morning, that
the time which had so perversely dragged last night was
now streaming past her at an accelerated and unreasonable
speed. "But this is my last morning on earth," she thought
with a sense of shock, and she jumped up and began looking for the pipes through which Señor Castigar would send
the gas. She found them in the wall under her cot and sat
down again. She realized that during the long night behind
her she had extracted from this experience everything that
could be squeezed from it and now she must have change
or go mad. Something alien was building inside of her: this

morning the cell's narrowness was so overwhelmingly and shockingly oppressive that she felt a savage urge to push back the walls, which she could in fact touch on either side of her without moving. She shivered. Her cell was already a coffin.

"I give you until one o'clock," he had said, and she glanced at the watch and saw that five minutes had passed. Slowly, deliberately she unstrapped the watch from her wrist, dropped it to the cement floor and ground the glass beneath the heel of her shoe. That terrible man Castigar— for the first time she saw him clearly and directed her thoughts toward him with malevolence. She remembered him saying, "You will learn soon enough that life is meaningless," and then, "You see? Even your courage was meaningless."

He dared to say that.

He dared.

"Damn him," she said softly, feeling a blaze of anger at his shrewdness. "Damn you," she said violently, and heard herself hiss through clenched teeth like an avenging witch. "Damn you to hell," she shouted, and the impact of her shout abruptly released her from submission and to her astonishment she felt like a hollow vessel slowly filling with rage.

She stood up, staring down at her body as if she had never felt it before and it was as if the rage she felt was rising in her like floodwater, filling every artery and vein until they pulsated and flowed red with it. In awe she lifted her hands and stared at them, watching them also become instruments of rage, the fingers curling into fists and tingling with aliveness. "But this must be what it's like to feel!" she cried in wonder. This current flowing through her, connecting her to every remote part of her self, reduced past angers to polite and tepid exercises, this was like the inner depths of a volcano slowly building into a rending eruption. And still the rage ignited her until she quivered with it and glared about for possibilities to spend it upon, for this luxurious and splendid fury had to be used or she would die.

Her eyes fell on the metal tray of food—she could kick

it to the farthest corner of the cell or she could bang on the door and viciously scratch out the eyes of anyone who dared come.

Neither was enough. It was not that kind of rage, it did not want to destroy but to assert.

Her eyes went to the window high in the wall. With this rage that possessed her she wanted to tear it away, free it, break it, in her rage she felt alive enough to assail the walls with her bare hands, climb even to that thin shelf on the right wall and hurl herself five feet across the cell to the window on the left wall.

Shelf . . . she had not been consciously aware of any shelf before.

Stop, Melissa, she told herself. Stop. Think. Wait.

No, no, it was impossible. The ledge was no more than an architectural accident, a deviation in the wall, and it must be twelve feet above the floor. Even if she could by some superhuman effort reach it, she couldn't possibly leap from there to the high window, which was on the opposite wall and slightly higher than the ledge.

Impossible . . . two men had already died here. He had said so.

Her eyes narrowed and she put her head back to scrutinize the window but from here she could see only that it was a small square opening set into the wall. It could be a window or an air duct; light came through it, and arrived in the shape of a perfect square so that presumably there were no bars or louvers. Why would they bother, after all, when the window was hopelessly beyond reach?

She turned to the right wall to look at the ledge, and then she stood on the cot to see better. On the cot . . . Her anger in abeyance, she looked down at the sheet of plywood and then jumped from it to examine it better. The plywood was not nailed in place; she discovered that it was only wedged tightly into metal inserts that protruded from the wall. With a feeling of awe she freed the plywood and lifted it out from the wall. If she could prop it against the side of her cell and use it as a kind of ladder, and somehow mount it, then six of the twelve feet between floor and shelf could be abridged.

If she could climb a smooth surface like plywood ... if the ledge was deep enough to give both hand and toe hold ... if she could hurl her body across five feet of space to catch at the window ... and if the opening really was a window ...

She replaced the plywood and stood on it for a wiser look at the ledge. Once it might have defined the spine of a chimney or held ornaments in a room no longer existing, or if this had once been an outside wall it might have been a touch of architectural cunning to cast a shadow across an otherwise bland stucco wall. It was a set-back beginning at the center of her cell and running across the wall into the cellar beyond; from this distance she judged the shelf to be anywhere from six to eight inches in depth.

Not very deep. Deep enough perhaps to hold a flower pot but surely not deep enough to contain a body that must somehow bend knees to stand erect enough to gather momentum for a leap through space.

But she could try at least—anger was better spent than wasted. Tentatively, trembling a little at her audacity, she up-ended the plywood again and wedged it against the wall, tested it and leaned her body across it, fumbling with arms and knees for leverage to climb. But there was no conquering such a smooth and slippery surface. She went to her purse to see what tools it might contain. Its contents were meager: a pencil, a wallet, a glass swizzle stick, compact, lipstick, comb, loose change, and bills. Her passport was in the hotel safe and her travelers' checks locked in her suitcase. What she did find was the toy flashlight with which she had read Emerson during the endless night just passed, and seating herself on the floor she removed the batteries and then the glass. Using the metal tube she gouged indentations in the plywood just deep enough to hold the toe of her shoe: four of them, like steps to the top.

Her anger was no less potent now but it was controlled, like a subterranean current feeding her vitality. Her mind was also controlled as it planned ahead with a stern efficiency. Without considering either success or failure she checked over what she might need for success. She would have to leave behind her trench coat and purse and probably her wallet as well. She removed a handful of pesetas from her wallet and rolled them into the taut left pocket of her cotton skirt. Into the right-hand pocket she slipped a few coins and Stearns' book: the book fitted with a snugness that pleased her. She next sat down with the breakfast tray and stoically ate cold omelet and drank a cup of cold coffee.

Now she was ready to try again. She braced the sheet of plywood, setting it almost vertically against the wall, and put her foot into the first hole and then the second, and had nearly approached the top when the weight of her body drew the plywood back until it fell, carrying her with it. Gritting her teeth with determination she placed the plywood back against the wall in a slightly more diagonal position. This time she approached the top without unbalancing the plywood but reaching the third toe hold she stopped helplessly, because there was nothing to grip with her hands, they were totally useless appendages against these smooth surfaces and once she reached the top of the plywood she would be so close to the wall that her nose would touch it. The ledge would still be six feet above her, and the closeness of the wall would hurl her back.

"Damn," she said aloud, and then it occurred to her starkly, bleakly, that to meet with any success at all she was going to have to use her body with the terrible ruthlessness of a tool, welding it to her intelligence until it obeyed her without anticipation of pain or damage. She thought with a tightening of her lips, "Very well then—did you expect this to be easy, did you expect it not to hurt?" She stepped to the top of the plywood and in the one precarious second given to her before the nearness of the wall rejected her she stood on tiptoe and touched—actually touched with her fingers—the rim of the ledge. A second later the rigid wall thrust her backward and she rolled and skidded down the plywood to the floor.

But she had touched the ledge—and if the next time she

gave a small jump, as much of a jump as she could manage without her knees striking the wall, she might hang from the ledge and discover her next move.

Up she went, and with a lift of her toes grasped the ledge with ten fingers and hung there—and tears came to her eyes as she understood that what she had to do next was to pull the trunk of her body up behind her, using only the muscles of her arms and nothing more. It proved agonizing as inch by inch she dragged her body out of the space in which it hung until her elbows rested on the ledge, trembling from the strain. Now she was halfway up but uncertainty overwhelmed her because to kneel on this ledge she must lift even more of her dangling body. With panicky eyes she gauged the depth of the shelf; it was far too narrow a space in which to turn herself around. The best that the ledge could offer her was another precarious toe hold for a jump, but how could she ever stand on this ledge? Having briefly rested the outraged muscles of her arms she used them again to pull her hips to the ledge, and for just one moment she experienced the satisfaction of kneeling on the shelf, and then she attempted to sit on it, her right hip moved too abruptly, and the wall literally pushed her off the ledge. This time she fell twelve feet.

She picked herself up, her body thoroughly jarred by the fall. Up the plywood she went again, balanced precariously for a moment on its upright edge, and, with muscles screaming, pulled her body up again until her elbows rested on the ledge, hesitated a second and then pulled her body higher. This time she succeeded in negotiating her hips to the ledge without tripping over the right arm that braced her, but now, sitting on the very edge of the shelf, she saw that this was not enough either, for her hands, her shoulders and her hips got in her way each time she moved. The wall was too close, the space too narrow.

Carefully, gingerly, she experimented with possibilities for standing. She turned just a little and placed one foot along the ledge. But again her shoulders were in the way and threatening to push her from the ledge if she moved farther. She began to cry a little with frustration as she sat there, one leg dangling and one leg along the ledge for she saw that there was simply no way to pull herself out of this sitting position. The next time that she mounted the plywood she must not stop to rest at all but kneel on the ledge facing the wall, and in her attempt to stand she would have to use the same movement of her body for the jump into space before the wall hurled her back to the floor. The wall would of necessity thrust her back but she must use this thrust for a momentum *up* rather than *down*.

This time, trembling from fatigue, she lowered herself down into the cell without falling. What she was attempting was insane—she knew this—and yet a possibility had opened up for her and she could not admit defeat yet, the idea was untenable, even as her mind told her it was inevitable.

She began all over again. It held within it now all the elements of a mad choreography, she thought: the steps up to the top of the plywood, the quick leap before the plywood could fall, the hands clutching the rim of the ledge, body dragging itself up with every muscle crying out in protest, the resting of elbows on the ledge, the knee placed on the ledge and then—

*"Now!"* she cried silently, and as she brought one foot to the ledge she recklessly spun on the rim of the shelf and using the momentum behind her pivot hurled her body blindly through space toward the window on the opposite wall.

She struck the wall just below the window, nearly stunning herself, and then she slid down the wall to the floor, her fingers clutching the stucco as she fell and leaving traces of blood behind them. Bruised and dazed she stumbled to her feet, brushed off her skirt and angrily mounted the plywood again: up, push, drag, rest, kneel—and resisting all thoughts of her bruised body she spun and leaped again. Up and across, and this time her fingers tantalizingly brushed the base of the window sill and for just a second trembled there, until the weight of her body carried her down to the floor of the cell again.

She lay there panting, and when she lifted her head and

looked up at the wall it was with hatred and revulsion, her
nerves shrieking in anticipation of new pain, her body pro-
testing new wounds. Doggedly she arose and doggedly she
approached the plywood. Up, jump, pull, drag, hoist, then
rest—but not too long, damn it, she whispered—and then
kneel and rest again—and then—

"Now!"

Again her fingers brushed the sill, clutched and lost the
sill and she dropped, sobbing, to the floor.

This time she fell on her side and lay there, all anger
spent, her body bruised and raw. She had to give up now, it
was absolutely pointless to make such efforts, it had to be
simpler to lie here and passively wait for the death that
would come in only a few hours. It would come with a
gentle hissing sound, she supposed, followed next by a
drowsiness and then—really it would be quite comfortable
for her—the beginnings of sleep. He really was humane,
she agreed, except that of course he was counting on her
fear of death to crush her first. But certainly his methods of
killing were kinder than her own, it was folly to stun herself to death like this, she could not remember what she
was trying to prove. There had never been any real hope of
succeeding.

Wearily she lifted her hands and looked at the blood
trickling down the palms, looked at the splintered nails and
ripped fingers. Her body trembled from the repeated
shocks of falling, her knees and elbows ached unbearably.
She put her head down on the floor again, ready to surren-
der both will and spirit to the inevitable, hoping that if she
closed her eyes she might sleep her way into death. A
manic fury must have driven her, she thought drowsily, but
she could no longer remember what had caused it, and now
her attempts appeared so absurd to her that she did not
know whether to smile or to weep. What on earth had
possessed her to leap like a crazed monkey from wall to
wall?

Rage had possessed her, she remembered, a rage begot-
ten by thoughts of Señor Castigar—it all seemed very distant and inconsequential now—and then she opened her

eyes, suddenly alert, as she realized that she had completely forgotten Señor Castigar. In her preoccupation, in the act of attempting to scale the unscalable, she had given not so much as a thought to Señor Castigar, or to Doctor Szym or to Stearns, or even to Adam, and this knowledge shocked her, it even frightened her so that she sat up in astonishment. She had assailed the wall of her cell because she had to, because she must, because there was nothing else to do and because it was necessary for her to try it. She had tapped a new strength, never before used.

She had done it for herself.

Not out of hope, for there had never been any real hope of success, and not to impress God or an unseen Stearns, or even to defy Señor Castigar, but for herself.

Something deep inside of Melissa stirred and trembled. She realized that in this cell she had lost everything—hope, despair, anger, illusion, personality, the past, and the future—yet she had lost nothing because in spite of being stripped of all these she remained, still, herself. Everything that she had depended upon for existence had been peeled from her layer by layer and yet she survived intact—she could *feel* this survival, she could feel the shining core that had never been touched by loss or by illusion or by time, she could feel within her the unknown that had terrified her the most of all—herself—and at this core she met and felt at last the pure steadying knowledge of what and who she was.

"I *am*," she whispered in astonishment, feeling the pieces of self interlocked and whole.

"I am," she repeated softly, feeling the rootedness of it, the separateness of it, the aloneness of it, the richness and joy of it, and she understood that she was touching reality at last, and that it was within her, not outside of her in the world or in anything that could ever happen to her in that world. Reality was here, in this moment, and she realized with a sense of wonder that the moment was all that she had ever possessed. There had never been anything else. There never could be. Each moment was a microcosm of life, containing in it the future as well as the past—it was the moment, not the future, that trembled with possibilities, with marvels of richness and depths that only a few dared to plumb. There had never been a future—except as illusion—there was only Now. And into this moment, into this now, she could still pour everything that she was and celebrate both herself and the life that remained in her, for if beyond this hour lay death then what was death except another Now, another place to enter, another Copenhagen or Paris to meet and make known. Once rooted like this she saw that the whole pattern of life changed, that the meager emotions to which she had been conditioned—excitement, disappointment, anticipation—held no possible meaning at all. For what could excite when everything— even to the falling of a leaf—was a tender experience, and what external circumstances could disappoint if one looked for nothing, having all within? It changed life from a series of unanchored and chaotic events into a mosaic where each experience—of varying depth and value—proved of equal proportion in the creation of a harmonious whole.

Why ask what life is, she whispered. It is.

Why ask what I am? I *am*.

Humbly, calmly, she rose to her feet and began to mount the plywood again, as she would continue to do for so long as she remained capable but not out of need or desperation or hope but because she was alive, and to be alive was to act, think, affirm, move, and create. Calmly she measured distances with the eye and performed her intricate choreography of life: up the board, jump, rest, kneel—but this time there was neither haste nor urgency for there was no longer anything to lose or to gain. She pivoted, jumped, arched her body through space and struck the opposite wall, clutched at the sill and held it again for just an instant with bleeding fingers before she fell heavily to the floor again, crying out in pain. But the next time she would do better, and perhaps before she died she might do even better: life could still be experienced when it was filled with intention. Again she dragged herself to her feet and went to the plywood and mounted it, jumped and held the rim of the shelf with her hands, pulled herself up, rested, pulled again, briefly knelt, and in the act of standing, spun and leaped—

. . . and to her astonishment clutched the sill and hung there, gasping at the pain in her hands, and then put aside her astonishment and with tired, sobbing slowness dragged up her body until her elbows met this sill, and then with only one more effort she rolled her body into the deep enclosure of the window.

She was in the window. *She had reached the window.*

And was to remain alive . . . The thought pleased her yet held within it no sense of great relief or of escape but rather it felt like a gift given her to be held lightly for new miracles, new possibilities. Slowly, persistently she drove her shoulder gently against the glass of the window, and as it broke she thrust her hand through the opening in time to catch the glass before it shattered on the sunlit flagstones beyond. For just a moment, poised on the verge of escape she looked back and down into the cell which she had occupied, seeing its smallness, its narrowness and its darkness like a skin that she was leaving behind. Then her head followed her hands and she looked out upon a long, fenced-in alleyway. The sun was brilliant—it was midday —and from a distance she heard sounds of traffic but listening heard no voices. Stealthily she crept through the jagged glass of the window and stood up and tiptoed down the alley and through a half-open gate at the far end. She found herself in a long garden facing another gate, with the house behind her. As if in a deep and tranquil dream she opened this gate, too, and walked into a street.

Sunlight glittered across pastel cement walls; flowers bloomed with unbelievable color and fragrance against white walls and at the end of the street a delivery van turned around and drove away. She moved toward that end of the street, to a boulevard filled with passing cars. At the edge of the avenue she paused, drinking in the air, the sunshine, the feeling of life. Once, long ago, when she had assumed escape was possible, she recalled—still as if in a dream—that she had placed pesetas, as well as Stearns' book, in her pockets. They were still there. It seemed that she was destined, after all, to deliver Stearns' book and this knowledge brought a rush of gratitude. When an empty taxi passed she lifted her arm.

*"Buenos días!"* gasped the driver when he saw her, and wrenched his cab to the curb.

Melissa looked down at her bleeding hands, torn skirt, and bruised legs. She said softly, "I have money. What time is it, please?"

He held up his wrist, tapping the dial of his watch with a finger and she saw that it was twenty-five minutes before one o'clock. She nodded. "I wish to go to the Anglo-Majorcan Export Company, please, at number eleven, Plaza Veri Rosario."

The man's eyes widened. "Not to a doctor? Not to a hospital?"

She shook her head and climbed into the seat behind him. "No, to number eleven Veri Rosario, please—and I think you had better hurry."

Suddenly she laughed. "I have been trying to get there for a long, long time—perhaps for all of my life," she told him, "but today I think I will arrive there."

"It is a drive of less than fifteen minutes," the man said reprovingly as he pulled out into traffic, honking his horn.

Melissa only smiled. There were some distances, she thought, that could never be measured by earthly means, and there were some journeys never to be found in any guidebook. . . .

## Dorothy Gilman and
## the Mrs. Pollifax mysteries

*Don't miss any of the adventures of
intrepid part-time CIA agent Emily Pollifax!*

—

THE UNEXPECTED MRS. POLLIFAX
THE AMAZING MRS. POLLIFAX
THE ELUSIVE MRS. POLLIFAX
A PALM FOR MRS. POLLIFAX
MRS. POLLIFAX ON SAFARI
MRS. POLLIFAX ON THE CHINA STATION
MRS. POLLIFAX AND THE HONG KONG BUDDHA
MRS. POLLIFAX AND THE GOLDEN TRIANGLE
MRS. POLLIFAX AND THE WHIRLING DERVISH
MRS. POLLIFAX AND THE SECOND THIEF
MRS. POLLIFAX PURSUED
MRS. POLLIFAX AND THE LION KILLER

—

*Look for Mrs. Pollifax's latest adventure!*
MRS. POLLIFAX, INNOCENT TOURIST
Now available in hardcover